"It's critical for my mom to have something to return to when she recovers. We have to make this work," Logan said.

"Yes, we do," Caroline said. Logan's determination was contagious. Strange, the compassionate and purposeful man she'd faced today didn't fit with the image she'd had of him any more than his broad shoulders and toned arms matched the boy she used to know.

Maybe she didn't know him as well as she thought she did, she acknowledged with a sheepish smile. But when he grinned back at her, his trademark dimples popping on his cheeks, Caroline's breath caught, and a ticklish feeling settled inside her belly.

"Are you all right?" he asked.

She nodded. But was she really okay? Something had to be wrong with her if she was reacting so strangely to Logan Warren. She wasn't usually fazed by any man, let alone a player with boyish charm and movie-star good looks. Hadn't she learned her lesson about men like him a long time ago?

Books by Dana Corbit

Love Inspired

A Blessed Life
An Honest Life
A New Life
A Family for Christmas
  "Child in a Manger"
On the Doorstep
Christmas in the Air
  "Season of Hope"
A Hickory Ridge Christmas
Little Miss Matchmaker
Homecoming at Hickory Ridge
*An Unexpected Match
*His Christmas Bride
*Wedding Cake Wishes

*Wedding Bell Blessings

DANA CORBIT

started telling "people stories" at about the same time she started forming words. So it came as no surprise when the Indiana native chose a career in journalism. As an award-winning newspaper reporter and features editor, she had the opportunity to share wonderful true-life stories with her readers. She left the workforce to be a homemaker, but the stories came home with her as she discovered the joy of writing fiction. The winner of the 2007 Holt Medallion competition for novel writing, Dana feels blessed to share the stories of her heart with readers.

Dana lives in southeast Michigan, where she balances the make-believe realm of her characters with her equally exciting real-life world as a wife, carpool coordinator for three athletic daughters and food supplier for two disinterested felines.

Wedding Cake Wishes
Dana Corbit

Steeple
Hill®

Published by Steeple Hill Books™

STEEPLE HILL BOOKS

Steeple
Hill®

ISBN-13: 978-0-373-87618-1

Recycling programs
for this product may
not exist in your area.

WEDDING CAKE WISHES

Copyright © 2010 by Dana Corbit Nussio

www.SteepleHill.com

Printed in U.S.A.

For everything there is a season, and a time to every purpose under heaven.

—*Ecclesiastes* 3:1

To all teachers who recognize and nurture their students' special gifts. Especially to my sixth-grade teacher, Alyce Stewart, who celebrated my love for words in front of the whole class, and to my high school newspaper adviser, Linda Donelson Spicer, who saw potential in me that I didn't recognize in myself. Your impact on my life and on those of your other students has been immeasurable.

Chapter One

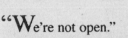

"We're not open."

Logan Warren tried to keep frustration from his voice. Someone had left the front door of Amy's Elite Treats unlocked, and now he would have to face his first customer before he'd even located the cake order forms. He almost asked himself if the day could get any worse, but the last week had proven to him that any day could. And had.

A few headaches at his mother's bakery were nothing, anyway, when compared to what Amy Warren was facing. Her image slipped into his thoughts. His mom looked so different lying in that hospital bed. The stroke had ravaged her body and stripped her face of expression.

Logan squeezed his lids shut and took a deep breath. She would survive—he realized how blessed his family was—but nothing could remove the mammoth lump in his throat, choking him from the inside out. He'd made a mistake in coming here this morning. He should have stayed at Markston Area Regional Hospital, continuing to keep vigil with his brothers. He should—

Logan stopped himself. She needed him at the bakery, too. Someone had to keep the business running for her. He'd been desperate to do something. Anything. It didn't matter that his mother made her living making wedding cakes and he didn't even believe in marriage. Running her bakery was one thing he could do.

Continuing past the huge ovens and industrial-sized mixers, he pushed through the swinging door to the dining area where bright May sunshine already poured into the store's windows.

"I'm sorry. We're not—" The word "open" fell away before he could speak it. "Caroline?"

Sure enough, the woman standing in the shop's doorway, finger-combing her mass of chestnut-colored hair, was Caroline Scott. He would have recognized her anywhere, even if her two younger sisters didn't happen to be engaged to, or married to, his two older brothers. And even if her high cheekbones and full lips didn't brand her as one of the Scott sisters.

She shoved all that hair behind her ears and lifted her gaze to meet his. "Oh. Hi."

"Hello?" The word came out sounding like a question because it was one. He rounded the counter to face the woman whose presence was no less perplexing than the unlocked door had been. Chicago was four hours from here. Would she have come all the way to Markston, Indiana, just to visit his mother at the hospital?

"You didn't say why…" Letting his words trail off, he indicated the room with a sweep of his hand.

"Oh, why am I here?"

Instead of answering his question, she stepped around the room, looking at the ice cream parlor tables and bakery cases as if they were the most interesting things she'd ever seen.

Now she really had him curious, even more so than when he'd been a nosy ten-year-old boy studying the *older woman* of fourteen. Caroline wasn't even the most beautiful among the lovely Scott sisters, but she was hands down the most intriguing. Even at twenty-eight, that hadn't changed. She had the most fascinating eyes, the darkest blue and almost impossible to read.

Those eyes turned back to him now and widened before she found something important to study on the tile floor. What was he doing staring at her, anyway? He had too much on his plate right now to be looking at any pretty woman, let alone Caroline Scott. *Unavailable* didn't begin to describe how out of the dating market her mother had said she'd been for years.

"This place looks great," she said, still not looking at him. "It's changed since the last time I was here."

"It's been a while."

"I guess it has."

She chuckled, gripping her hands together in a gesture that seemed uncharacteristic for the take-charge Caroline he remembered. Come to think of it, many things about Caroline were different today. She wore jeans and a T-shirt when she was usually a khakis-and-sweater-set type, and her hair was loose down her back instead of in its usual too-tight bun. Where were the intensity and confidence she usually exuded like perfume?

"You know, we don't open for another two hours," he said to fill the awkward silence. "Someone must have forgotten to lock the door—"

She dangled the keys in front of her to explain how

she happened to be inside the building. The door hadn't been left unlocked after all.

"I don't understand." And then he did. At least he thought he did. "They couldn't have."

But because it was entirely possible that his mother and Mrs. Scott *had* been up to another one of their schemes, Logan rolled his eyes. The two best friends were notorious matchmakers who'd had this crazy idea of arranging marriages between Trina Scott's three daughters and Amy Warren's three sons. Crazy like a fox maybe. Because God had a sense of humor, their matchmaking plans hadn't turned out exactly as they'd expected, but they could still claim two successes. Matthew and Haley were happily married, and Dylan and Jenna were engaged.

Could his mother and Mrs. Scott have planned a ruse to bring their last two single children together and have forgotten to cancel it in the chaos following his mother's stroke?

"Oh, I don't think—" She stopped herself, but her cheeks flamed a pretty pink.

"It shouldn't surprise us, you know."

Caroline stared back at him. He knew he should look away, but he couldn't. Though he had yet to turn on the overhead lights, electricity filled the room. From the way her pupils enlarged and she chewed her bottom lip, he could tell that she sensed it, too.

"Logan, that's not why I'm here."

"What?" He blinked, trying to clear his thoughts.

She worked the keys between her fingers. "Mom asked me to help you run the bakery until your mother gets better."

"Right. I knew that." He swallowed, trying to look

as natural as possible for a guy who'd just made a fool of himself. That was what he got for letting a pretty woman distract him from more important matters.

"You didn't think…?"

"Of course not." But he *had* thought Mrs. Scott and his brothers supported his offer to run the bakery alone, and he'd been wrong about that, too. "Our mothers would know better than to try that matchup. City-girl corporate climber with Nature Boy, as you've called me?"

She chewed her lip, but she didn't snap at the bait as he would have expected. Witty banter was standard fare in their two families.

"They should know better." She breathed an audible sigh of relief. "I promised to put myself up for adoption if they ever even thought about trying to set me up again. After being set up with both of your brothers, I've hit my lifetime quota."

She was agreeing with him, but her apparent relief that their mothers weren't matchmaking annoyed him. The look between them that she'd made no effort to break, the black of her pupils as they'd stretched over her blue irises. Since when did he misread the signals of attraction, anyway? Usually his instincts with women were spot-on—and he'd dated enough of them to know—so it baffled him that this time he'd read the signs all wrong.

As if she'd already forgotten the uncomfortable moment, Caroline stepped toward the display case again and studied the price list on the wall. "We'll have this place in shape in no time."

Logan sighed. Wasn't it enough that he'd practically had to arm-wrestle his brothers, a pregnant sister-in-law and a future sister-in-law for the opportunity to run the bakery? It exhausted him to think that Mrs. Scott's other daughter was going to argue with him over the job, as well.

"Look, I appreciate your coming all the way from Chicago, but I have things under control here."

He expected an argument, so her sad expression surprised him.

"I was sorry to hear about your mom's…illness."

"Stroke," he corrected.

"Right. Stroke." She winced at the word. "Mrs. Warren's an amazing lady. I'm sure she'll be just fine."

"Thanks."

The tears in her eyes convinced him not to mention the long rehabilitation his mother had ahead. It touched him that Caroline seemed to really care about his mother. And even if what she'd said was a platitude like those so many others had spoken this past week, he desperately wanted to believe she was right. He just wanted his mother back.

"Well, you'll probably want to get to the hospital for visiting hours. Mom will love seeing you." He paused, searching for the right words to show her he appreciated her compassion even if he didn't need her help. "Would you like me to call your mother and let her know you're coming?"

"But my mom said—"

Because she stopped herself, Logan guessed he wouldn't appreciate whatever her mother really had said. "Caroline, I'm sorry you went to so much trouble, taking off work and all to come here—"

"It wasn't any trouble."

Clearly, she wasn't going to make this easy. He

cleared his throat. "Anyway...I hate that you've wasted your time, but your mother must have misunderstood what we needed here. I already took leave from my job, and I want to do this for Mom."

"Since we're both here, why don't we work to-gether?"

"Together? Like a team?" He tilted his head to study her. "I hate to tell you this, but you're not the best team player. You have to be captain or camp counselor or even head honcho like you are at that mega-mall."

She coughed into her hand. "I'll just stay until you get your sea legs. That would be okay, wouldn't it?"

Logan stared at her. "Why are you insisting on this? Your mother probably had to beg you to take off time from work, and now I'm letting you off the hook."

"I don't need to be let off the hook. I'm letting *you* off the hook. Isn't this messing with your busy social calendar, anyway?"

"Nothing could be more important than this," he said. "How did you get time off, anyway? Your mom's always complaining that you hardly ever can get away from work."

"Well, I did this time," she said and then cleared her throat. "And I happen to have a lot of experience with running a business. You know, purchase orders and employee benefits and such. Just like you have in your type of job. All the outdoorsy stuff you do as Ranger Logan."

Logan couldn't keep his jaw from tightening, but this wasn't the time for him to clear up her confusion about his job because he had a more important point to make. "So, exactly how many wedding cakes have you made?"

"Uh...none."

"Just as many as I have."

This time she rolled her eyes at him just the way she used to when they were kids and he told one of his knock-knock jokes. "You don't have to be able to decorate the cakes to run this kind of business."

Logan tapped an index finger against his cheek. "So I should do just fine by myself."

"Why are you being so stubborn? You're being just like you were when you were six, and you didn't want to wait for your turn for board games. It's almost June, the biggest wedding month of the year in Markston, and you're wasting time arguing with me instead of working with me."

She took a few steps toward him, pinning him with a look that would have made him straighten up and fly right when he was a kid. But because they were adults now and he towered over her, Logan only stared her down.

"Yes, I know what June is." He didn't try to hide his irritation. "I've been around this business a long time. You're wasting *my* time when I need to be getting up to speed on things. I told Mom I would do this, and I'm going to do it...alone."

She fisted her hands at her sides. "You must be the most infuriating person who ever lived."

"No, I think there are two of us."

"I think you're both right."

At the sound of the third voice, Logan turned to look at the glass door that Caroline had unlocked. Trina Scott stood just inside it, her crossed arms over her chest.

Logan sighed. None of the employees had even arrived, and it was already looking as if he wasn't cut out for the job he'd promised to do. But his brothers, Mrs. Scott and even Caroline were wrong to doubt him. Somehow, with God's help, he planned to make this work.

Caroline stared at the floor avoiding her mother's gaze, her cheeks burning. She was so shaken that several seconds had passed before her pulse slowed. It didn't make sense. In the business world, she'd always been cooler than a cucumber on ice. No one had been able to get a rise out of her. Now, infuriatingly stubborn Logan Warren had done it without breaking a sweat.

Why couldn't he just be gracious and accept the help he so obviously needed? In a bakery, a park ranger would be like a bull in a china shop anyway. But instead of being grateful for her offer, he'd insisted on asking questions about why she had the free time to come to Markston.

She'd hoped in the confusion regarding his mother's health crisis that no one would have time to wonder about her sudden availability. She hadn't expected Logan Warren to be the observant type, but nearly as soon as he'd seen her, he'd zeroed in on the point she'd most hoped to hide.

What surprised her even more was she'd been tempted to share her whole humiliating story with him. Something about the way he'd studied her with those bright green, penetrating eyes had made her wonder if he could see how lost she felt. Maybe he understood because they shared that feeling of uncertainty in common.

"Will one of you explain what's going on here?"

Her mother's words pulled Caroline back from her strange thoughts. Where had they come from, anyway?

Logan had enough on his mind with his own family crisis for him to concern himself with her problems. And for her to imagine that she had anything in common with ne'er-do-well Logan Warren demonstrated just how off-kilter she'd been the last few days.

"It was nothing," Logan answered for the both of them. "Just a disagreement."

"I can see that." Trina tucked her chin-length brown hair behind her ears with all the care of someone who had a huge mane of it—or someone waiting for a better answer.

"What are you doing here, anyway?" Caroline asked.

"Refereeing apparently. I had hoped you two would work this out together, but…"

That her mother was standing inside the bakery rather than the hospital's critical care unit made it clear she hadn't trusted the two of them to find a way to work together.

"Sorry, Mom."

"I'm sorry, too." As Logan bent his head, his light brown hair fell across his eyes. "I know you were trying to help when you called Caroline, but—"

Trina shook her head to interrupt him. "Logan, stop right there. Your mother's facing the crisis of her life, and all you can do is spend time arguing about whether you need my daughter's help at the bakery?"

"I'm not trying to upset you, Mrs. Scott, but I have this under control. I already took leave from work." He gestured toward Caroline. "We don't both need to lose time at our jobs during Mom's recovery."

"That won't be a problem." Trina glanced sidelong at her daughter. "You didn't tell him, did you?"

With heat scaling her neck and face, Caroline shook her head.

Her always matter-of-fact mother took a step toward Logan. "Because of the current economic downturn, investors pulled the financial backing on the Ultimate Center, and the whole project for the mega-mall that Caroline managed folded."

"You lost your job?"

Caroline looked up to find Logan watching her. She pressed her lips together and nodded.

"I'm sorry to hear that."

"Thanks." His compassionate tone made her shift where she stood. Vulnerability was a new feeling for her, and she doubted she would ever wear it well.

"As soon as Caroline told me what had happened at work, I knew this would be perfect. God definitely has a plan here."

"God wanted your daughter to lose her job?" The side of Logan's mouth lifted.

"Oh, you know what I mean." Trina waved away his usual attempt to be a class clown with a brush of her hand. "So it appears that you're both available to work here, at least for a while. And it's going to take both of you."

He appeared to consider what she'd said. "Go on."

"Okay, Logan, your heart was in the right place when you volunteered to run the bakery, but you don't have any business experience. Caroline has that, so it's a blessing that she also has an abundance of free time right now."

"Thanks, Mom." Caroline slid a glance Logan's way and was relieved he wasn't watching her now. Her mother had managed to praise and offend both of them at the same time.

"Just telling it like it is." Trina held her hands wide. "And, Caroline, though you have more business experience than he does, Logan is more invested in *this* business than you are. He'll do whatever it takes to make sure the bakery survives."

"She's right," Logan said. "I will."

"Even if that means putting up with my daughter being here to do it."

Logan opened his mouth, but he must not have been able to argue with that logic because he closed it and nodded. "Mom needs to have something to return to when she recovers. No matter what, we have to make this work...for her," he said after a moment.

"Yes, we do," Caroline agreed. The vehemence in her voice startled her, but she couldn't help it. His determination was contagious. Strange, the compassionate and purposeful man she'd faced today didn't fit with the image she'd had of Logan any more than his broad shoulders and toned, tanned arms, clearly of a man who worked with his hands, matched those of the boy she used to know.

She smiled to herself as she realized that maybe she didn't know him as well as she'd thought. But when he grinned back at her, his trademark dimples popping on his cheeks, Caroline's breath caught, and a ticklish feeling settled inside her belly.

"Are you all right, sweetheart?"

"What?" Caroline jerked, caught daydreaming for the second time in a single conversation.

"Are you going to be okay to handle this project?"

"Of course I will."

But was she really okay? Something had to be wrong with her if she was reacting so strangely to Logan. She usually didn't let any man faze her. Certainly not a guy who was four years younger than she was. Absolutely not a player with boyish charm and movie-star good looks. Hadn't she learned her lesson about men like Logan Warren a long time ago?

She pushed away painful, private memories with a shake of her head. Whatever was going on inside her, it had to stop right now. She'd just promised to help Logan learn to run his mother's business, and she couldn't do that if she allowed herself to be distracted. The answer to that challenge was simple: in order to help the *baker,* all she had to do was to ignore the *baker's son.*

She peeked at Logan again and this time found him watching her, seeing too much. Swallowing hard, she looked away. She realized with a shock that ignoring Logan Warren would be easier said than done.

Chapter Two

Caroline glanced up from the drawer where she'd been mentally cataloging baking tools only to find that the two cake decorators she'd met earlier were studying her just as intently.

"You're Trina Scott's daughter, aren't you?" the red-head named Margie asked, squinting as if she hadn't quite placed her.

"Yes, I am."

Come to think of it, Logan had introduced Caroline only by her first name when he'd updated the staff on his mother's condition and on changes at the bakery. After that, he'd slipped off to his mother's office with the excuse of learning the accounting software. Well, at least one of them could avoid curious glances from the staff.

Figuring it was time to take charge, Caroline stepped toward the stainless-steel counter where the women sat on stools, working on their masterpieces. "Do you know my mother?"

The women looked at each other and laughed.

"Do we know her mother?" Margie asked her cohort

as she spread chocolate buttercream frosting over a sheet cake.

Their laughter was enough to make a person nervous.

The stout brunette named Kamie paused from her task of stretching a sugar dough called fondant over a three-layer yellow cake. "Even if we didn't already know Trina since…oh…second grade, we would have known her from here at the shop."

"Oh. Right."

Her mother probably spent more than her share of time at Mrs. Warren's business since moving back to Markston. Caroline could only hope that it hadn't been so much time that she had been tempted to share family stories.

Margie shook her frosting-covered spatula at Caroline. "You're the one who's decided not to marry."

"I—" Caroline frowned. Definitely too many stories. She needed to establish professional employer-employee boundaries with the staff here…and fast.

"You sure messed with your mother's and Amy's matchmaking plans before they realized they were targeting the wrong bride," Kamie said, chuckling. "But they figured it out, didn't they? They got your sisters matched up just right."

Her face felt like it was on fire. She needed no reminders of those humiliating matchmaking events, where the two moms had tried to set her up first with Matthew and then with Dylan. It didn't matter that she'd never planned to marry or even that she was thrilled that both of her sisters had found love. She still couldn't help feeling sensitive over all of that rejection.

The decorators were staring at her, curiosity painted

all over their faces. If someone asked her if she was married to her career, Caroline was sure she would die of embarrassment. What was she supposed to say now? That she and her career had divorced? It wasn't anyone's business, any more than anyone needed to know that her choice not to date was less about her feminist leanings and more about a broken heart.

Caroline braced herself, waiting, but the two women were suddenly studying something behind her. She didn't have to turn to know that Logan was back there, witnessing the whole humiliating exchange. The tingling at the back of her neck gave her enough of a hint.

"Just thought I'd check in and see how the cakes were coming along."

Logan leaned against the wall just inside the kitchen doorway, his arms crossed. His words were innocuous, but his jaw was tight, and his fingers pressed too tightly into the snug-fitting cuffs of his short-sleeve polo shirt. His words were layered with meaning, as well. It couldn't have been clearer that he thought the decorators should spend more time decorating cakes and less time looking for information on Caroline's personal life.

Margie must have gotten the message because she bristled. "They're coming along just fine, *Mister* Warren."

"Well, that's great to hear, *Margie*." He put as much emphasis on her first name as the decorator had on his title since she'd avoided using his given name. "We'll all have our work cut out for us with Mom out of commission."

"We'll keep that in mind," Kamie said in a banal tone.

Caroline couldn't help staring at Logan. Had he really

just stepped in to defend her? Inexplicably, a memory from last Christmas sneaked into her thoughts. It was one of Logan with chilly rain plastering his flannel shirt to the wide expanse of his back as he hefted an ax to take down his mother's massive Christmas tree.

What was wrong with her? She couldn't be flattered that he'd come to her rescue when she had every right to be offended. She was no damsel in distress any more than Logan was a knight in shining armor. Or Paul Bunyan.

"Things are going great out here," Caroline said to fill the uncomfortable silence. "How's everything in the back office?"

"It's a slow start, but I'll figure it out."

The two women, who seemed to be making a point of not looking at Logan, exchanged a look.

"Of course you will," Caroline couldn't help saying. Whether Logan should have stepped into the conversation or not, she could see that it had put him in an uncomfortable position with two of the employees on the first day. The least she could do was be gracious over his sacrifice if he would have to deal with that awkwardness. "There's a learning curve to working with new software."

"Hopefully, the hill won't be too steep. I didn't bring my climbing gear." He chuckled at his own joke though no one else joined him.

"You know I could give you a few pointers—"

Logan raised his hand to stop her. "Thanks, but I'll figure it out." He turned back to the employees. "Well, carry on, ladies."

Without waiting for a response, he returned to the office but closed the door only halfway.

"Sorry if we were too...er...invasive," Kamie said as soon as he was gone, and her partner nodded her agreement.

"Thanks." Caroline almost wished they'd apologized to Logan instead.

"We've just heard so much about your two families since your mom moved back to Markston that it's hard not to get caught up in the stories," Margie said with a shrug. "Especially the matchmaking part."

Caroline slid a glance toward the open office door, from where Logan had to be able to hear the conversation. Whether he'd denied it or not, he'd guessed that their mothers had been trying another one of their matchmaking ambushes. Could he have been right? She hated admitting that she suspected it, too, but she hated even more that her palms dampened at just the thought of it.

"Well, it's good that you'll be here helping Logan," Margie began again. "He'll need it."

Again, Caroline's gaze darted toward that open door, and she was even sorrier this time that Logan could overhear them. Okay, she'd doubted his abilities herself when her mother had said he would be operating the bakery during his mother's recovery, but she hated that no one seemed to be in his court.

"Logan would have had this place in shipshape in no time. With or without any help."

"Of course," Kamie said.

Her comment must have surprised the women as much as it had Caroline because both gave her guarded looks before turning back to their cakes. She told herself her small show of support was only to help Logan establish himself in a position of authority so he could manage the business. At least, that was the only way she could explain it.

Caroline returned to her own task of familiarizing herself with the kitchen tools. After she closed the last drawer, she glanced up at the clock and stepped down the hall to the office. Through the crack in the door, she could see Logan crouched over his mother's laptop and tapping keys at an angry pace. He must have sensed her presence, because he turned back to her.

"Do you need something?"

"I was going to offer again to help you out with that software program."

The side of his mouth lifted. "No. Really. I'm good. If I don't figure it out soon, I'll call for help."

"Okay, I guess," she said.

Caroline didn't even know why she was belaboring the point other than that she felt indebted to Logan. First, he'd taken pity on her and agreed to work with her *after* he'd learned about her joblessness, and then he'd come to her rescue with the busybodies. She wasn't used to feeling beholden to anyone, and it didn't sit well.

She had to make it up to him; that was all there was to it. She would already have done that if he would only allow her to give him a computer mini-course.

Well, she would just have to find another way to return his favor. Maybe she could teach him how to do inventory lists or complete supply order forms. She didn't care if she had to learn to operate the giant mixers just so she could teach him how to mix up a yellow cake batter. In the next few days, she would find something to do so she could settle her debt to Logan Warren.

"Well, that's just not good enough."

The sound of the screeching female voice reached

Caroline's ears the moment she stepped inside after her quick lunch trip home to drop off her luggage. She'd been sure that when she returned to the bakery wearing her business-casual ensemble of black slacks and a crisp white blouse the rest of the day would be a breeze. Wrong.

"I don't want *one* wedding cake," the woman continued, her voice still a few decibels above a speaking voice. "I want each of my guests to have an individual cake."

"Of course," Logan said in an unnatural-sounding voice. "Multiple cakes do make a statement, but I'm not sure, based on the budget you've just presented me, that they would be the best choice."

Caroline cringed as she hung up her purse on the hook next to Logan's black leather jacket and motorcycle helmet. She hurried into the kitchen, where several employees were crowded near the swinging door. Had Logan never heard of the business adage, "the customer is always right"?

Since none of the employees were bothering to hide the fact that they were eavesdropping, Caroline didn't pretend, either. She leaned close and spoke out the side of her mouth. "What's going on out there?"

"Just another Bridezilla with big ideas and too small a wedding budget," Margie told her.

"Why isn't anyone helping him?" But as soon as she asked it, Caroline realized she didn't want anyone else to do so. She'd been looking for a way to repay Logan for stepping to her defense earlier, and this was perfect. She knew how to appease irate customers with her eyes closed and both hands tied behind her back.

Squeezing past the decorators and two cake bakers,

she pushed the swinging door open. Through the glass in the bakery counter, she could see Logan seated across from the furious bride-to-be.

"Well, you'd better find a way to make it happen, or I'll be taking my business elsewhere. Amy's isn't the only bakery in town, you know."

Certain the deal was heading south faster than a flight from Indianapolis to Orlando, Caroline skirted around the counter and hurried toward the table where Logan sat, staring down at the price binder instead of at his customer.

He looked up and lifted a hand to stop Caroline, but she ignored him. He might not be happy about this now, but he would thank her later when she saved him from losing a customer on his first day at work.

"What Logan was about to say is that we at Amy's Elite Treats would be delighted to work with you to make a cake or cakes that will meet all of your needs and impress your wedding guests."

As the young bride looked up at her from the binder of wedding-cake photos in front of her, Caroline took a few steps forward. "Hello, I'm Caroline."

The young woman brushed at a few angry tears and then looked back and forth between Caroline and Logan, as if she wasn't sure which one she should be listening to.

"So you will be able to make individual cakes for all my guests and stay within my budget, too?"

The woman must have chosen her as the primary source now because those red-rimmed eyes appeared hopeful and were trained right on her. Suddenly, Caroline felt as if she was walking into a business meeting unprepared—something she'd never done in her life.

Why had she jumped in with two feet before she even knew how deep the water was?

"Well…" she said, stalling.

"Go ahead, Caroline. Tell Nicole your plan for helping to make her wedding picture-perfect," Logan said.

"It's just that I'll need to check a few things first." Because Caroline was cringing inside, waiting for him to call her out in front of the customer, his chuckle surprised her.

"Come on. Don't hold back." He tapped his finger on the price list, speaking to the young bride instead of to his temporary coworker. "She was about to make a suggestion, and she's right. It would be perfect."

"What would be perfect?" the bride asked.

"You'll have to forgive me because this is my first day and I'm only familiarizing myself with the price list."

The vibrant, white smile Logan trained on the young woman could have earned a presidential pardon, as far as Caroline was concerned. She wondered why she'd never noticed before that the dimple in his right cheek was deeper than the one on his left. Why she was noticing it now, she didn't even want to analyze.

"Anyway," Logan continued, "I'm sure Caroline had already figured this out, but we have an alternative in the price list that will fit into your budget and still make a statement for your dream wedding." Logan maintained eye contact with the customer while he spoke, morphing into a confident salesman in a naturalist's body.

It didn't surprise Caroline that Logan would rely on his masculine charm to smooth over the situation, but that he'd used it to cover her gaffe—now that surprised her.

"How would you do that?" the bride asked.

"You could have a small two-layer cake for the wedding party and then provide mini cakes, which serve two people each, for the other guests." He glanced down at the price list and then back up at her. "Another option would be to have a cake for each reception table, but just by ordering mini cakes you'll be cutting your number of cakes in half and trimming some of the cost."

"It's up to you," Caroline joined in, "but if I were one of your wedding guests, I might like the warmth and community of sharing cake with a friend." She didn't look at Logan, but she could feel his gaze on her.

The woman thought for a few seconds and then nodded. "I guess that could work."

"It'll be great. You'll see," he said.

Having won the bride over, Logan made an appointment for her to meet with one of the designers early the next week and walked her to the door. Caroline had bent to return the photo albums to the shelf behind the counter when she realized he was standing behind her. She straightened and turned to face him.

"You just couldn't help yourself from coming to my rescue."

"No— I mean, I didn't—" Finally, she gave up and shrugged. She couldn't deny it because that was exactly what she'd been doing.

Instead of answering, Logan stepped around her and pushed through the kitchen door. Caroline trailed after him, relieved that the eavesdroppers had had the good sense to scatter.

He announced to the others that he would be taking his lunch but didn't even look back at Caroline as he switched into his riding boots, grabbed his helmet and jacket and headed outside. The door had barely closed before the sound of his motorcycle reverberated off the concrete walls.

He had every right to be mad. She might as well have worn a firefighter's helmet and carried a flashing red light as obviously as she'd tried to rescue him. Only, he hadn't needed rescuing, and he'd ended up covering for her. She didn't know what to do with that truth.

She listened, waiting for the roar of the motorcycle engine to filter away, but instead, the sound stopped. Seconds later, Logan stomped into the entry, carrying his helmet under his arm. Strange how he didn't look the part of Matthew and Dylan Warren's little brother as he stood covered in all that leather gear and indignation.

Caroline drew in a breath, not entirely from shock.

"I need to talk to you," he said, lowering his helmet to the floor. He glanced around at the employees who were pretending not to listen. "Outside," he added.

Swallowing, she followed him, and when he held the door open for her, she didn't argue. Under normal circumstances, she would have considered telling him she was uncomfortable with such chivalrous notions, but the tight set of his jaw told her this wasn't the time.

As soon as the heavy steel door closed behind them, he whirled to face her. "Why did you do that?"

"I don't know what you—"

But Logan didn't let her finish. "You know exactly what I mean. You showed up like the cavalry, planning to save the day, and you did it in front of the whole staff. As if they weren't already doubting my abilities."

"It's just like when were kids and you fell off your skateboard and…" She blew out a breath. "I was just trying to help."

"No, you were just disappointed that I didn't fail."

She shook her head. "That's not true."

He paced to his motorcycle, shoving his hands back through his hair. "I knew I was making a mistake. I knew it."

Though he'd been speaking more to himself, he turned back to her now. "I get it that you agreed to come here because you thought you could do a better job running the shop than I could. If I hadn't felt sorry—" He stopped himself but not before his message became clear.

Caroline drew in a breath. Just because she'd suspected he'd only accepted her presence out of pity didn't make it any easier to hear the truth spoken aloud.

"I didn't mean that."

"Yes, you did."

He started to deny it, but one side of his mouth lifted and the steel of his posture softened. "Okay, I sort of did."

"And you're kind of right about why I came here. I also had quite a bit of free time." She shrugged and then met his gaze directly. "But you're wrong about me wanting you to fail. I just wanted to pay you back—"

Logan drew his brows together. "Pay me back?" Realization must have dawned because he started nodding. "Of course. I got the ladies to stop before they started asking a bunch of nosy questions, and you're trying to return the favor."

"It's good that you understand."

"You mean how crazy it would make a control freak like you to be indebted to anyone? Sure, I understand."

"Thanks, I think."

"I knew that some of the employees were listening from behind the door."

Caroline stared at him. "You knew? I'm sorry that they don't seem all that supportive of you."

"It's always tough when the boss's kid takes over."

"Well, that's unfair of them to discount you before they've given you a chance."

"Is that so?"

At his smile, she felt ashamed. Wasn't that exactly what she'd done? "Sorry."

"No problem."

"You didn't need my help, anyway. You were amazing with that bride."

He studied her, as if waiting for a punch line. "Thanks," he said finally. "Look, why don't we just call it even? We don't have to keep score for the next few weeks. I'll even try to listen to your suggestions while you're here, preferably if you don't give them in front of the other employees. And you can…"

"I don't know…trust that you know what you're doing until you ask for help? And maybe you could avoid mentioning my being…er…unemployed around here."

"Deal."

His smile was so warm that Caroline was convinced she could feel the heat on her own skin, but she tried to shake away the thought. This was just the invigorating feeling of having a purpose again. That had to be it. If not, she was in big trouble because her immunity to Logan Warren was in danger of falling faster than a cake after someone slammed the oven door.

Chapter Three

Logan trudged along the tiles of the same hospital corridor he'd paced so many times in the last few days, the antiseptic scent stirring nausea in his belly. Caroline's footsteps tapping in time with his only unsettled him more.

As if visiting with his mother this way wasn't heart-breaking enough every time, it was even harder seeing the shock on friends' faces the first time they visited. None of them saw any hope for Amy's recovery, no matter how much lip service they paid to it later. He could just imagine how bleak Caroline's expression would be. She tended to see the world in blacks and whites with little hope for grays.

"Will your motorcycle be okay where we left it?" Caroline asked from behind him.

The uncomfortable look on her face when he glanced back at her probably had more to do with the critical care unit they were about to enter than the fact that she'd insisted on driving when they'd left work, but he nodded anyway. He would have declined her offer of a ride, but then he would have been forced to consider why he'd needed to put space between himself and this particular woman. He didn't want to touch that with a ten-foot pole.

"The bakery's in a pretty safe neighborhood. Even if the door really had been unlocked this morning, the store probably would have been fine."

The last he'd added to calm her nerves, but she was too busy staring at the sign that said "Critical Care" to notice his effort. He stopped just outside the department's double doors, with his hand on the button that automatically opened them.

Caroline paused beside him. "Has she been conscious?"

"Most of the time. She'll be glad you came."

Caroline's gaze darted to the door and back, and then she straightened her shoulders. They entered the department and Logan turned at the first hall.

"It's down this way." After a week of visiting, he could have found her hospital room with his eyes closed.

Next to him, Caroline was fidgety and nervous, the same way she'd been at the bakery that morning. And then he remembered the likely reason for her disquiet. Caroline had lost her father two years before, and hospitals probably reminded her of that loss.

Well, they shared that discomfort with hospital settings in common. Just as he had during every visit, he felt as if he was coming out of his skin, and they weren't even inside his mother's room yet. He paused just outside the door.

"It's going to be okay," he said, for his benefit as much as hers.

He could tell from Caroline's sharp intake of breath the exact moment she saw his mother lying asleep in the second bed of the double room. He could barely keep himself from gasping every time he saw his mother this way.

In sleep, his mother's face was relaxed, but so far at least, her face became no more animated even when she was awake. The silver hair, which was rarely out of place, now stuck out all over her head and appeared to have turned white overnight. Her left arm rested tightly against her torso, her fingers curling back toward her body.

For several seconds, Caroline just stared, and then she took a few steps toward the bed. Over her shoulder, she whispered, "She's sleeping. Do you think we should go?"

"Wha…" Amy's eyes blinked open. She looked back and forth between them, her gaze filled with confusion. "Lo…"

"Yeah, it's me, Mom. Logan," he answered before she could struggle further. "Caroline's here, too."

The movement was small, but Amy managed to turn her head toward her best friend's daughter.

"Goo…"

"Yes, Mom, it is good."

He looked to Caroline then, but her stricken expression was gone, and the smile that replaced it could have made even the sickest person feel better. Rather than hang back as some of his mother's other visitors had, Caroline rushed forward and dropped a kiss on top of that matted head of hair.

"Oh, Mrs. Warren, I'm sorry I haven't made it here to see you yet." Lowering into the seat next to the bed, she reached around the bars to grasp Amy's good hand. "Are you feeling any better tonight?"

"Pea…"

"Mom, I sure hope you're saying that you're feeling 'peachy' and not like 'pea soup.'" He crossed to the opposite side of the bed and bussed his mother's cheek before returning to take the seat next to Caroline.

"Bo…th," Amy said with obvious effort.

Logan and Caroline chuckled over her comment that sounded humorous whether she intended it to or not. Caroline lifted up from the seat and leaned in to brush the hair back from Amy's face. Logan pretended not to notice that as she did it she blinked back tears, but he swallowed the emotion thickening in his throat.

When Caroline lowered into the chair again, she gestured with her head for him to take his mother's hand instead. An unsettling feeling squeezed in his chest, and his eyes burned. He drew in a gulp of air and let it out slowly. Tears wouldn't give his mother back the full use of the left side of her body or her ability to speak. He believed that prayers could, but he wished God would hurry up with His healing power.

They sat for a few minutes longer, watching as Amy nodded off. There was something comforting about Caroline being there, someone who cared for his mother almost as much as he did. This compassionate side of Caroline was new to him, seeming to soften her hard edges, but he suspected that side had always been there, buried beneath all of her goals and lists.

The sound of footsteps brought his attention to the door. Mrs. Scott pushed the door open, a paper cup in her hand.

"I didn't realize you two were in here. Dylan and Jenna are in the waiting room. They'll want to come in when you're finished."

"Oh. Okay." He lowered his mother's hand and stood.

Trina stepped to the bed and lifted the pitcher off the side table, pouring ice water into the cup and replacing the lid and straw. "Did everything go okay at the shop today?"

Next to Logan, Caroline stood up from the chair, sending him a worried glance.

"We did fine," he said.

Caroline blinked but seemed to recover from her surprise. "Logan did a great job handling a difficult customer. You would have been impressed."

It was Logan's turn to be surprised, but before he had the chance to look over to Caroline to see if she was serious, his mother shifted next to him.

"Shop?"

Amy had just awakened again, and already she was asking about her business.

"The bakery is going to be okay, Mom. No matter what it takes, it will be there when you're ready to come back."

Caroline looked his way then. Her gaze touched him in a warm, steady connection. She didn't have to say anything aloud for him to understand what she meant. He'd made a commitment to his mother, and she'd stepped forward to help him keep it.

As Logan sat in one of the folding chairs squeezed around Trina Scott's small dining room table, he couldn't help thinking that something was wrong with that picture. In fact, everything was wrong with it.

The Saturday-night dinner should have been around his mother's mammoth dining room table. As always.

She would have insisted on doing all the cooking and would have managed to top her last amazing meal. As always. This was his mother's domain. Her fifty-plus-hour weeks making desserts for other people's families should have taken away the novelty of preparing food for others, but she lived for dinners like this one. That only made it more tragic that she might never be able to host another one.

Logan pushed the thought from his mind. He should have been starving for a good meal. When was the last time he'd eaten anything that hadn't been wrapped in cellophane? Still, he found himself pushing meat sauce and ricotta around on his plate.

"It's not quite the same, is it?"

Logan looked up to find Mrs. Scott studying him from the other side of the table. She glanced at his plate of nearly untouched lasagna and then back to his face.

"No, the food's great. Really." He took a big bite to reinforce his comment but had to follow it with a gulp of iced tea to choke it down.

"You can't kid a kidder, son."

"It does seem strange, I guess."

"Whew," Haley called out as she reentered the room, her folded arms using her pregnant belly as a resting spot. "I thought nobody was going to say it. No offense, Mom. Your cooking is great, but having a Warren-Scott dinner anywhere but in Amy Warren's dining room just seems wrong."

Murmurs of agreement came from the others crowded around the table. Logan smiled at his sister-in-law, who pressed her hand to her back while she lowered herself into a chair. The two of them hadn't agreed on much over the years, but they were in complete agreement on this one.

"I miss Grammy," Lizzie said as she rounded the table and climbed up in her aunt Caroline's lap.

"We all do, sweetie." Caroline wrapped her arms around the child and pressed her cheek to Lizzie's.

The movement of brushing her fingers along the little girl's braids in a comforting touch appeared surprisingly natural for a woman who was probably more comfortable in a boardroom than anybody's living room. But then Logan remembered the Scotts' unusual family dynamic. Because Mrs. Scott wasn't comfortable with emotional scenes, she often sent Caroline to deliver hugs as her surrogate.

He'd heard all the stories about Caroline comforting Haley after she'd been dumped by her fiancé and wiping away Jenna's tears after she'd messed things up with Dylan. He'd just never witnessed these things himself until the last few days, and he was having a tough time reconciling this person to the businesswoman who'd marched into the bakery and tried to take it over.

Logan didn't realize he'd been staring at her until she glanced over and caught him. He turned away in time to find Matthew watching *him*.

"Now, Logan, I would have expected you to be the last one to show up to joint family dinners," Matthew said. "You were amazingly talented at finding ways to avoid them."

Logan understood that his brother was only trying to lighten the serious mood in the room, but it didn't make him feel any less guilty over what Matthew had said. Still, he tried his best to play along with the joke. "Could I help it if I had a date?"

"When didn't you have a date?" Jenna supplied.

He didn't mind that they all had a laugh at his expense. They needed a reason to laugh, and the reasons had been precious few the last few days. Out of his side vision, he caught sight of Caroline watching him, and he couldn't help wondering what she saw.

"I did a pretty good job of avoiding family dinners myself," Dylan said. "Optometry conferences, you know."

"All because you didn't want to see me." Jenna elbowed her fiancé and then, linking her arm with his, smiled down at the diamond solitaire on her hand. "Both of you were also trying to avoid the matchmaking schemes."

"I never missed any of those dinners," Matthew said. "I am the good son, after all."

They all shared another laugh at that, and Haley reached over to ruffle her husband's hair. "Those were some good times," she said in a wistful voice.

Matthew took her hand in his. "Yeah, good times."

Trina planted her hands on the edge of the table with a thud. "Stop it, all of you. The last thing Amy needs is for you to be thinking this way, as if she's not going to be able to do any of things that made her happy. She will be fine, and she doesn't need any of you naysayers holding her back."

"But none of us said—" Caroline began, but she cut her words short when her mother frowned her way. She lifted her hands in surrender.

Trina turned back to Logan. "And, Logan Warren, don't you worry. You'll have plenty of chances to avoid your mother's amazing dinners for dates with your blonde-, brunette- or redhead-of-the-week."

They were laughing at him again, but at least they were laughing.

Trina pressed her hands together as if to signal that the earlier subjects were closed. "Now how did things go at the bakery today?"

Automatically, Logan shot a look at Caroline. She was staring back at him.

Dylan leaned forward and rested his hands on the edge of the table. "Go ahead. Tell us. Was it as bad as the other day? We heard you two were arguing outside the back door. We would have direct quotes, but no one could hear through the steel door."

"You heard wrong," Logan grumbled.

"That's the same story I—" Matthew started, but Caroline cut him off.

"It was pretty quiet today since we had no wedding cake orders this weekend."

"No weddings on Memorial Day weekend?" Trina said.

Logan looked up in surprise and noted that Caroline had reacted the same way. Clearly, he wasn't the only one who'd failed to notice they were in the middle of a holiday weekend. They wouldn't be celebrating the beginning of summer with a cookout this weekend anyway.

Before Caroline could answer for the two of them again, Logan spoke up. "You know how small Markston is. Some weekends Mom has three weddings to bake for and other weekends, none at all."

"We're booked for every weekend in June," Caroline added. "As long as new orders are coming in for fall and not going to Cakes & More instead, we're fine."

Scoffing sounds came from around the table.

"That name isn't spoken aloud around here," Logan explained. "That place has been a thorn in Mom's side for the last six years."

Trina snapped her fingers. "So that was what Amy was trying to tell me at the hospital today. She's worried about the competition."

"She doesn't need to worry," Logan assured her.

"Oh, she knows that, sweetie. She's just keeping the business in her thoughts as her brain heals. She's processing all those memories as she works her way back."

Works her way back. Trina's words reverberated through Logan's thoughts. Had he been praying for his mother's recovery without really believing it could happen? The question convicted him in a way that even thoughts of his empty seat at all those family dinners hadn't.

It was difficult for him to imagine his mother entertaining big crowds or running her fast-paced business when so far she hadn't even mastered her aim for lifting her fork to her mouth, but he couldn't allow himself to think that way. Who was he to limit his mother's recovery or God's ability to heal? Faith was about believing without seeing, and his mother needed them all to believe.

"Is everyone ready for dessert?" Trina asked as she pushed back from the table.

"I am," Lizzie announced.

The adults just stared at each other. Matthew's daughter was too young to understand, but the others couldn't forget that Amy Warren's scrumptious cakes were a tradition at every Warren-Scott family gathering.

Not having them there didn't feel right. Logan caught Caroline's gaze, and she gave him a sad smile.

"You know, Mrs. Scott, I'm pretty full already," Logan told her.

Trina had started toward the kitchen, but she turned back. "Oh, that's too bad. My brownies are cooling on the counter. I thought we'd put scoops of vanilla ice cream on top." She paused, resting her knowing gaze on Logan. "Are you sure you're too full?"

Logan pushed back from the table and patted his belly. "Oh, I think I could fit a little."

"Good." Trina took orders from the others and continued into the kitchen.

No one mentioned the cakes or their absence, but Logan was grateful Mrs. Scott hadn't purchased one of his mother's desserts for the occasion. She understood that the effort for continuity would have hurt more than it soothed.

Soon they were all gushing over Trina's brownie dessert and laughing together about old times. That, too, was a Warren-Scott family tradition.

Logan smiled as he thought how much his mother would hate missing tonight. But there would be other times, he was suddenly certain. His mother would even host her infamous dinner parties again. He just knew it. And when she did, he would happily attend every one.

Chapter Four

The pews were only half-full at Community Church of Markston that Sunday morning, reminding Caroline again that it was a holiday weekend. As odd as it felt for her to be sitting in her mother's church, she would have felt just as out of place at her own church in Chicago as seldom as she'd darkened its doors lately.

With Jenna and Dylan on one side of her and Haley and Lizzie on the other, Caroline couldn't resist peeking farther down the pew to her mother. She fully expected one of her mother's knowing stares, cueing her in that Trina had guessed about her sporadic church attendance. She hadn't exactly given up her faith, but she'd had a hard time squeezing church into her Sunday work schedule.

But Trina wasn't paying attention to her at all, her focus on the doors at the rear of the sanctuary. Suddenly, it made sense. Mrs. Warren had always been annoyed by Dylan and Logan's continual tardiness at church. Jenna had reformed Dylan, but Logan was probably still playing beat-the-church-bell. In Amy's absence, Trina must have seen it as her duty to censure Logan.

At the front of the sanctuary, Matthew sat in his music minister's seat, his focus on the back door, as well.

"He's not going to make it," Jenna said, glancing at her watch.

"I should have called him before I left my apartment," Dylan murmured.

Jenna chuckled. "Don't worry. My mom will make him toe the line."

"Like you did me?" He took her hand.

Caroline shifted in her seat. She'd never noticed before how many family jokes were directed at Logan. About small things from his Casanova ways to his job as "Ranger Logan," but they all came with mild disapproval for his choices. Had he taken on the role of the family comedian to deflect some of that?

Her sudden temptation to tell both of their families to knock it off made her smile. Logan would not appreciate her defending him. He didn't need her to be his champion now any more than he'd needed her to step in when he'd been dealing with that difficult customer. She understood that he was fine on his own, but that didn't keep her from watching the door and rooting for him to show up *tout de suite*.

Just as the organist played the first notes of the processional music, Logan breezed through the door, a weathered leather Bible tucked under his arm. Although most of the men in the sanctuary wore polo shirts and slacks, Logan was dressed like it was Easter Sunday. He'd paired his navy suit with a crisp white shirt and a blue tie with geometric designs in the exact green shade of his eyes.

"What?" Logan asked in a low voice as he came to

the end of the pew. His left eyebrow lifted in question, that same side of his mouth rising, as well. "Good morning, everyone."

He might have said *everyone,* but he was looking right at Caroline. Only then did she realize she'd been staring at him with her mouth hanging open like a landing pad for flies. She clicked her teeth shut and shifted again. It didn't matter how amazing he looked; she had no excuse for staring. But a glance around told her she wasn't the only one who'd noticed the man who wore a business suit with the same ease as he sported jeans and hiking boots.

Logan didn't pay attention to the fuss as he waved to Matthew up on the podium and scooted into the pew next to Caroline's mother. As Trina reached over and patted Logan's arm, Caroline couldn't help thinking of the service last Christmas when her mother and Mrs. Warren had made a display of standing and shifting seats so that she and Dylan were forced to sit together.

Caroline hadn't really expected her mother to try something like that this morning, but she couldn't explain her mild discomfort when she didn't. She should have been relieved. Was she disappointed that her mother and Mrs. Warren hadn't tried to set her up with a *third* Warren brother? That couldn't be possible.

Her gaze slid to Logan's end of the pew. No, not possible, she decided, choosing to ignore the annoying seeds of doubt that lingered.

"Let's get this morning started off right," Matthew said as he stepped to the lectern. "I can't imagine a better way than by singing 'How Great Thou Art.'"

Caroline smiled up at her brother-in-law, grateful to him for interrupting her strange thoughts. This was what she needed to clear her head: good hymns, good meditation and a thought-provoking sermon on grace or the destructive power of sin.

But when Reverend Leyton Boggs directed everyone to turn to a passage in Mark Chapter 10, her hope faltered. It was the same passage she'd read aloud for Haley and Matthew's wedding.

"Jesus is a real proponent of marriage," Reverend Boggs began. "Not the temporary kind like we see so much today but the enduring kind."

He read from the beginning of the chapter, but when he reached Verse 7, Caroline found herself quoting the Scripture with him.

"'For this reason a man shall leave his father and mother and be joined to his wife, and the two shall become one flesh,'" she whispered.

Looking up from her open Bible, Caroline glanced at the couple seated to her right. Dylan was cradling Jenna's hand and moving it so that the sanctuary lights caught on the facets of her diamond engagement ring. Soon those two would be "one flesh." Caroline looked up in time to catch Matthew and Haley exchanging a warm look. They already had melded their lives into one.

A knot formed in her throat, surprising her. Her gaze moved again to Logan on the opposite end of the pew. Did their siblings' cozy togetherness ever make him uncomfortable, the way it did her? More than that, did their obvious happiness ever make him wonder if he was missing something like—

No. She cleared her throat, uncrossing and then re-crossing her legs. Logan wasn't the settling-down type any more than she was. If he was committed to anything, it was to playing the field. And her life was complete. Not a thing was missing. But had she been happy, even before she'd received the pink slip? Had she truly been fulfilled? Did she have real friends or just colleagues? She praised the joys of her solitary life, but sometimes wasn't she just lonely?

"I don't need a wrap-up when Jesus said it so well for us in Verse 9," the minister said when Caroline finally tuned back in to his message. "'What therefore God has joined together, let not man put asunder.'"

Reverend Boggs had taken his sermon full circle back to the passage in the Book of Mark. Her thoughts had been just as circuitous, but unlike the minister, she had no answers to her questions. Clearly, her job loss was causing her to rethink all her choices, but was it more than that? As much as she didn't want to admit it, her general ennui just might have something to do with a park ranger who was trying his hand at running a bakery.

After Reverend Boggs spoke the benediction, Caroline had the urge to make a break for the parking lot. But how could she explain her sudden need to avoid spending time with the two families she loved most in the world? Or that she wanted to avoid a particular Warren family member?

Because there was no way she would admit any such thing, she followed Dylan and Jenna into the center aisle and braced herself for the crush of another Scott-Warren family reunion.

Lizzie reached her first, wrapping her arms around her skirt-clad legs.

"Church is over, Aunt Caroline," she announced.

"Did you think I was good in church? Mommy and Daddy let me have dessert after lunch if I'm good."

Caroline reached down and tugged one of the child's sandy-brown braids. "You were great in church. I think you deserve two desserts."

"Just one will be fine," Haley said as she reached them. "Thanks for the help, Caroline."

"Anytime."

Dylan elbowed Jenna and leaned close to speak to her in a loud stage whisper. "Remind me not to let your sister anywhere near *our* kids."

As she laughed, Caroline felt herself relax. It was always like this when their two families got together—a lot of silliness, plenty of jokes. One marriage, another engagement and even a serious health crisis hadn't changed that. Maybe nothing had changed.

But as Logan came around the front of the pews and stepped into the circle next to her, his sleeve brushing her bare forearm, tingles raced to her shoulder. Something was different in the old family-friend circle, all right, whether she cared to admit it or not.

Dylan grinned at his brother. "So, Logan, did you have a job interview after this, or just a photo shoot with *GQ?*"

"Oh, this old thing?"

"I think he cleans up nice." The words were out of Caroline's mouth before she had the chance to censor them. To keep from fidgeting, she tucked her hair behind her ear. Why did she always fidget so much around him, anyway?

He lifted an eyebrow, but then he grinned. "Thanks. You, too."

"Thanks." She brushed her damp hands down the

sides of her black pencil skirt, careful not to touch her silk blouse and leave embarrassing handprints. "Remember the time when we were kids and your mom had cleaned you up for church only to find you rolling down the hill in the backyard?"

As soon as she said it, she was sorry, but she couldn't seem to help herself. She'd always joked with Logan as much as the others.

"I'll try to remember not to roll on the ground today," he said, his voice sounding tight. "I wonder to whom Reverend Boggs was speaking with his message this morning."

Caroline stilled her hands on her hips. She deserved that, she supposed. But when she looked up again, he wasn't talking to her. He had sidled up to Dylan instead and was patting him on the back.

"Sorry, everyone." Dylan held his hands wide. "Jenna and I didn't mean for everyone to be included in our premarital-counseling class."

Trina had been over talking to a few of the church ladies, but she approached in time to hear the last. "If you're starting counseling, does that mean you two have finally set a wedding date?"

"Mother, please." Jenna rolled her eyes.

"We'll get around to it," Dylan assured her.

"I'm not getting any younger, you know," Trina said, her lips in a pout that earned her a laugh.

No one mentioned Amy, or that she was a few years older than Trina and that her health was precarious at best, but the awkward pause in the conversation showed that they were all thinking about her again.

"You know…if you were to set a date, it would give Amy something to look forward to." Trina held her hands wide as if to show the simplicity of her idea. "It would give her another reason to work to get home sooner."

"I don't know, Mrs. Scott," Dylan said, shaking his index finger at her. "Are you worried your most recent match won't make it to the altar?"

"Of course not." She waved away his suggestion. "I just know that Amy would want you all to live your lives instead of putting them on hold while she's recovering."

"That's just what I've been trying to tell *you*, Mom," Haley piped in. She moved between her sisters. "Did she tell you guys that Mr. Kellam invited her out for coffee, and she shot him down? The poor guy."

"Why, Mom?" Jenna asked. "Frank Kellam is a cutie with all that silver hair and those blue, blue eyes."

"Yeah. Why not?" Caroline wasn't sure she was ready to see her mother begin dating, but she didn't want her to be alone, either.

"Would you all hush?" Trina looked flustered as she shot a glance to the rear of the sanctuary. "He's a member here, you know."

"He's really nice, too," Jenna said.

Trina gave Jenna a warning look and turned back to Haley. "Now I told you…even before everything with Amy…that it wasn't going to happen."

"Why not?" Haley rested her crossed arms on her belly. "Dad died more than two years ago. You should—"

"Not long enough." Trina shook her head. "It will *never* be long enough."

A second uncomfortable silence settled in the sanctuary, until Logan started chuckling. Everyone turned back to see what was so funny.

"Well, well, well, Mrs. Scott," he said finally. "It's different when the tables are turned, isn't it?"

Instead of answering, Trina stared at him waiting for him to explain himself.

Logan held his hands wide, as if the explanation was simple. "The matchmaker gets a dose of her own medicine, and it doesn't taste too sweet."

All the younger adults laughed, but Trina gave him one of those looks that used to hush her daughters in church.

"There will be no matchmaking, and that's final."

"Okay," Logan said with a shrug. "But you might want to remember that Matthew said that same thing. And Haley. And Dylan. And Jenna."

By the time that he'd made it through the list, Jenna and Haley were muffling giggles, and Logan's brothers were looking away, trying and failing to cover their smirks.

"Logan Michael Warren," Trina said in the same warning tone that they'd all heard Mrs. Warren use after one of Logan's jokes.

When Logan stiffened at the sound, Caroline couldn't help but do the same. Everything had to remind him of his mother lately.

But when Caroline turned back to her mother, Trina was smiling in a reminder that all thoughts of Mrs. Warren didn't need to be sad ones.

"Since Amy couldn't be here today, I knew she would want me to pick up the slack."

Laughter filled the sanctuary again, with Lizzie

laughing the loudest in that way children do when they don't get the joke.

Just as Matthew returned to them from the receiving line in the vestibule, the overhead lights flickered off, leaving behind only the yellow cast of daylight filtering in through the stained-glass windows.

Matthew pointed to the lights. "There's our signal to go home. Unless you all just want to stay until the evening service."

"Back to my house, then?" Trina looked around at all their faces. "Chicken and noodles are in the Crock-Pot, and a pie is cooling on the counter. We'll eat a nice lunch and then head over to visit Amy."

After several affirmative murmurs, they all started up the aisle toward the exit.

Logan cleared his throat just as they stepped outside. "Ah, I don't think I'm going to be able to make it."

"But—" Trina's smile fell.

"I'll catch up with all of you at the hospital."

Dylan elbowed his brother and waggled an eyebrow. "Got another date?"

"Something like that," Logan answered.

"Who with this time?"

Logan shrugged but didn't answer.

"Guess he's not telling." Matthew glanced at his watch. "It's barely past noon on a Sunday, bro. That has to be a new record for you."

Haley stopped and faced her husband. "Jealous of all that freedom?"

"No way. Not me." Matthew held his hands up in a defensive pose.

"Good answer," Haley said with a grin.

Caroline told herself she wasn't jealous, either. Not

of Logan's hopping social calendar. Certainly not of the woman who would be spending the afternoon with Logan, though she was curious about this mystery woman. Knowing Logan, she was probably beautiful. And equally empty-headed.

No, Caroline definitely wasn't jealous. But disappointed? She shouldn't care one way or another whether Logan spent the afternoon with her—um…their families, but she did. Her excuse that she only wanted them all to be together didn't hold water, either.

How could she admit that she wanted to spend more time with Logan Warren? Even if she were in the market for a relationship, which she wasn't, Logan was about the last man on earth she should choose, and yet something was drawing her to him.

Something that needed to be stopped. This was a recipe for disaster, especially with the two of them trying to work together. It didn't matter how handsome he looked when those dimples popped or how he made her laugh with his clever repartee. She was a strong, independent woman—not some hopeless romantic. She had to admit she was attracted to Logan, but she planned to get over it right now.

Logan set his helmet on his motorcycle and threw his head back, closing his eyes and breathing in the earthy scent of southern Indiana. Though Boyton County State Park was more crowded than he preferred with holiday picnickers and the air was tinged with the scent of barbecue grills, serenity still flooded Logan's veins.

Even the twenty-minute ride out to the park on his Harley hadn't made him feel so at peace. He didn't need people in this place, could be alone without feeling lonely. He was at home.

Sunlight warmed his face and filtered through his closed lids, transforming darkness to an orange glow. The heat made his leather jacket uncomfortably warm, though, so as he opened his eyes, he shrugged out of it. He hooked his thumb under the collar and tossed it over his shoulder.

Just twenty paces from the gravel parking lot, he reached his favorite spot. From the lookout, he had the best seat in the house to see God's creations in the verdant valley below and the rolling hills in the distance. A robin chirped on a nearby sycamore tree branch, and a hawk swooped below, hinting at even more wildlife hidden beneath the backdrop of green.

Tossing his jacket on a grassy spot near the drop-off, he settled next to it. He stretched out his legs, crossing his booted ankles, and rested back on his elbows. Instead of bowing his head, he tilted his chin up and closed his eyes.

"Father, I feel Your presence here," he prayed aloud, without worrying he might be overheard. "Thank You for holding Mom in Your hand all week. Thank You for carrying all of us through this difficult time. I ask that You continue to hold Mom, to heal her if it is Your will."

Logan didn't say "amen" because he and God still had a lot of talking to do today. Their chats here tended to take a while. A smile pulled at his lips as he wondered what his brothers would have thought if they knew this was his "date." What about Caroline? Would she be surprised?

He didn't know about that, but she was sure shocked

when she'd watched him roll into church in his best suit.
Had she liked what she'd seen? He'd sure appreciated
how lovely she'd looked in that narrow skirt and that
ruffled turquoise blouse—more than he should have.
She'd even worn her hair down again in a mass of waves,
and it had been all he could do not to brush his hand
through that silky chaos. Even now...

Startled, Logan straightened. Where had that come
from? He hadn't dressed up to impress Caroline, anyway,
had he? He shook his head hard. He'd made the effort
for his mother, whether she was there to see him or not.
Still, part of him couldn't help being pleased that he'd
gotten a reaction out of Caroline as well, even if it was
shock.

"Lord, why can't I get her out of my mind? Even
here."

Was he thinking of her because of Reverend Boggs's
sermon today? She'd seemed so uncomfortable after-
ward that he'd felt this strange need to shield her from
whatever was bothering her. It was absurd to imagine
that Caroline Scott would ever need anything from
anyone, him in particular, but he'd still felt it.

With a huff of frustration, Logan lay back on the grass
and stared up into the huge expanse of puffy cumulus
clouds. Even turning down Mrs. Scott's lunch invitation
to put some distance between him and Caroline hadn't
been enough to remove her from his thoughts. Her image
had just slipped inside his helmet and had come along
for the ride.

Well, he'd come out here to find some perspective,
and that was what he intended to do. He might have
allowed women to distract him so many times before,
but this time would be different. He intended to keep his

promise to his mother, and that meant avoiding all distractions, even those with brains and beauty to match.

He wasn't really attracted to Caroline anyway, he told himself. She was too different from him, her frenzied need for more and greater success as foreign to him as her life in the big city. Still, he couldn't help being intrigued by all of that intensity, all that drive. He liked to observe her the way he recorded data about some of the wildlife in the park. He didn't feel drawn by the vulnerability that only he could see in her. He was no more interested in her than she was in him.

"It would never work out, anyway. You probably never created two people who were more different," he said, chuckling. "She's Type A to the tenth power, and I'm—"

He stopped himself, squeezing his eyes shut. Who was he trying to convince…God or himself?

Chapter Five

Caroline had never thought of herself as claustrophobic, but as she stood inside the closetlike storage room with its walls appearing to creep in by tiny increments, she had to wonder.

She glanced down at the clipboard in her hands and then back up to the shelves nearest the ceiling. Logan had surprised her by showing up to work the holiday with her, instead of taking the day off with the rest of the staff. She would have said that he was the hardest-working wastrel she'd ever met, but she'd already decided that most of her preconceptions about Logan had been way off the mark.

At least they were working on separate projects, so they wouldn't be in each other's way or close enough to make each other uncomfortable with the rest of the staff gone. She chose not to wonder which of them might be more uncomfortable.

Instead of wishing this time that he would ask her for help on that laptop, she was grateful for his combination of excessive pride and limited computer skills. He would stay in that office for hours trying to figure out the program so that she could deal with the inventory and supply orders alone.

Already, she'd completed counts on the parchment paper and foil and then flour and sugar on the lower shelves, so all that remained were the supplies on the top shelf.

Pulling the step ladder from its hook on the wall, she set it on the floor and started up the steps.

She'd settled on the step where she could reach the huge containers of baking powder and baking soda when she heard a knock on the door just two feet behind her.

"Caroline, are you still in there?"

"Wait—"

But she didn't say it loudly enough because Logan was already pushing the door open, and the metal door struck the ladder with a thwack. The ladder took that as signal to dump its load—namely her.

"Oh, no," Logan called out as he stuck his head and arm in and grabbed one metal leg of the ladder. It might have been a gallant gesture if she weren't already sprawled on the concrete floor, her clipboard next to her head. Holding on to the ladder so it wouldn't fall on her, he pushed the door the rest of the way open and stepped inside.

"Sorry." He grimaced as he looked down at her. "Are you all right?"

"Ouch." Caroline sat up and rubbed her scraped elbow, but her backside had taken the brunt of her fall, and she wasn't about to let him know *that*. Heat flooded her cheeks, but she supposed she shouldn't waste time feeling embarrassed. She'd been nothing but vulnerable from the moment she'd arrived back in Markston.

"I'm fine. I would tell you to learn to knock, but you did that."

Letting the door fall closed behind him, he crouched next to her and reached out a hand. "Next time I'll wait for an answer."

As soon as his fingers closed over hers, Caroline realized her mistake in letting him help her to her feet. A tingle she couldn't define began in her fingertips and raced up her arm. His hands were callused from hard work, another contradiction in an endless line from the earlier image she'd had of him. For a fleeting moment, she wondered how it would feel for their fingers to be laced together, his rough thumb brushing on the back of her hand.

Caroline jerked back so quickly that she bumped the shelf with her sore elbow, but she managed to stay on her feet this time. She chewed her lip as she bent to collect the clipboard and pen from the floor.

"You sure you're okay?"

"Just trying to get my equilibrium back." Because it wouldn't be in her best interest, she didn't mention that merely being in his presence threw her off balance.

He glanced at the floor-to-ceiling shelves on one side of the room and the cleaning-supply closet on the opposite side. "I used to hide in here when I was in elementary school, but I don't remember it being so cramped."

A nod was the best she could manage with him so close that she could breathe in his fresh-scented bath soap. A four-foot buffer separated them, but it wasn't enough. She'd imagined that the room was shrinking before, but it was nothing compared to the cocoon of intimacy she felt now, the kind that made the tiny hairs on the back of her neck stand on end.

She cleared her throat, resisting the urge to rub her neck beneath the bun. "You were small for your age back then, and you probably weren't hiding in a group, either."

"Things have changed, I guess."

She swallowed. He was right, but she wouldn't be sharing that with him. Her plan to will away her attraction for Logan was working about as well as a car starting without an engine.

"Well, aren't you glad you chose this as the way to spend your holiday?" He glanced at the inventory sheet in her hands. "Nearly being maimed and all?"

"I needed to get out of Mom's house for a while."

"That's got to be cramped. Your mom wasn't planning for more than one houseguest when she bought her two-bedroom home."

"And Jenna has dibs on the guest room until the wedding—whenever that is—so I'm stuck with the sofa."

"Did your mom complain about you working the holiday?"

"Not really. I would have worked it at…er…my former position, too. Holidays and Sundays are the best for working without interruptions."

"I couldn't believe it when you asked Mom about working Sundays here." He stopped and shook his head. "That was about the clearest 'no' we've heard from her since the stroke. She's always been adamant about not working on the Lord's day."

"I didn't mind working Sundays. I wrote most of my reports on Sundays."

Logan tilted his head and studied her. "But didn't

you go stir-crazy holed up in that office while all the other people were with their families? Didn't you get lonely?"

Like she had been several times lately, Caroline was convinced Logan could see right through her. That he somehow knew that she worked at least part of the time because she had nothing better to do. She didn't want or need his pity. She straightened, feeling more insulted for that than any injury to her backside.

"Sometimes you have to make sacrifices if you plan to succeed in the business world."

He answered with a nod. She waited for him to point out how little good all of her sacrificing had done when it came time for layoffs, but he didn't say more.

She cleared her throat. "Uh, you never said what you needed from me when you came in here."

The side of his mouth lifted. "Just wanted to wish you a happy Memorial Day."

"Are you kidding? You nearly broke my neck, knocking me off the ladder for—"

"Me? Kidding?" He flashed his hundred-watt smile.

Instead of asking again what he needed, she lifted an eyebrow and waited.

"Oh, right. I wanted to see how you were doing with the inventory list."

"Fine. Sure there's nothing else?"

Logan shrugged, an embarrassed smile spreading on his face. "Okay, you've got me. That computer is giving me nightmares, so I'm finally bowing to your expertise. Will you help a poor Nature Boy in crisis?"

Caroline had to laugh when he looked at her with that theatrical expression and with his hands gripped together in a plea. She would have hugged him, too, for dropping the uncomfortable subject of her workaholic tendencies, but she figured that would just reignite tension of another kind. This room was far too small for that.

"Wow, humility and everything," she said, still chuckling. "It takes a strong man to admit he needs help. That's almost as amazing as a man asking for directions."

He'd already opened the door again and was leaning against it, but now he raised both hands in a signal for her to stop. "Whoa. Whoa. Let's not take that giant leap. I wouldn't want to disturb the real-man code by stopping at a gas station and asking for…the 'D' word."

"Don't worry about your membership in the guys' network. Your secret's safe with me."

He swiped the back of his hand across his forehead. "That's a relief." He started through the door but looked back at her. "Well, are you going to help me or not?"

"Of course, I am."

"Are you going to remind me every day that I had to ask you for help?"

"Me?" She did her best to look offended. "You think I would do something like that?"

"Well…"

Okay, she might have done that in the past, but if Logan could call their situation *even* when he'd had a clear advantage, she could be just as generous. "I'll try to hold back, then."

With a glance up at the top shelf and then to the stepladder she would have to brave again later, she started for the door. She paused as Logan stood holding the door open for her.

"Why do you always do that?"

"What?" He looked confused at first, but then he nodded. "Oh, you mean holding doors for ladies? It's a habit. Why? Does it offend your feminist sensibilities?"

"No," she said, bristling. "It's just unnecessary. I'm fully capable—"

"Well, that's just too bad."

She looked up in surprise, only to find him grinning at her.

"Sorry. But you don't know how much time my mother spent *instilling* that habit in my brothers and me." He smiled over some memory he didn't share. "You wouldn't want Mom to hear that I was anything less than the perfect gentleman working here, would you?"

Caroline tried to answer, but only managed to produce a strangled sound, so she cleared her throat. This was silly. He'd only told her about how his mother taught him proper manners, and all she could do was to imagine Logan opening doors and pulling out chairs…for her. Worse than picturing those things, she was enjoying the musings a little too much. What was wrong with her?

"Fine," she said finally and pushed past him to lead the way to the office. She was relieved to escape the cramped storage room anyway. She needed to step away from Logan and from his questions about her life in Chicago and about her life in general. It was exhausting feeling so transparent.

But as she turned into the office, she realized her respite was only temporary. Logan had already placed two chairs together in front of the desk. He moved past her now and took the folding chair, leaving the rolling desk chair for her.

Taking a deep breath, Caroline started toward the desk. Now the two of them would have to squeeze in front of his mother's laptop in another cramped space while she helped him master the software. Was there no place at Amy's Elite Treats that wasn't so cramped? She shook her head as she curled her hand around the external mouse. She was getting the feeling that no space was big enough for her not to feel the pull of Logan Warren.

Logan whistled a tune as he parked his motorcycle, digging through his pocket for the bakery keys. Today promised to be a great day. The sun was shining, the skies were clear, and his mother had spoken a full sentence on the phone to him this morning. He wouldn't even let it bother him that her all-important instructions had been to "work early on Saturday."

He had this work thing under control now. Over the past few days, the staff seemed to have fallen into a comfortable routine, beginning each day with him unlocking the doors and ending with him locking them again. He'd managed to fit in regular hospital visits as well, sometimes during lunch and sometimes after work.

But as he climbed off his bike, he had the sinking feeling that something was off. Until then he hadn't noticed several cars already parked in the lot, but now they were there as signs that he'd dropped the ball. Saturday, of course. That was what his mother was trying to tell him. Though the shop closed early on Saturday afternoons, the kitchen also opened early when they had wedding cake orders.

Breaking into a jog, he crossed the parking lot to the other side of the building. The door was propped open, and a chorus of voices filtered from inside. Great. As if the staff didn't already think he was the boss's incompetent son, he'd just proven them right.

He trudged down the hall, barely stopping to prop his helmet on the shelf, hang his jacket and change from his riding boots to work shoes, before hurrying into the kitchen. The room was hopping, with decorators and bakers already hard at work. Even two part-timers were working along one of the empty counters, making nothing but rosettes and hundreds of tiny green leaves.

"Hey, you're early," Caroline, who was coming in from the dining area, called out when she saw him.

Logan pressed his lips together. She'd probably had a heyday, sharing jokes with all of the staff. "Sorry—"

Caroline kept talking as if he hadn't spoken. "I was just telling the staff that you had business this morning, so you'd asked me to open for you." If she noticed his surprise, she didn't let on. "Did you finish everything you needed to do?"

Logan couldn't help but stare. It was like before. She was covering for him again, but this time she was doing it without letting the others in on it. Good thing they'd already agreed to call it equal because he would have owed her big-time for this one.

"Well, did you?" she pressed.

He cleared his throat. "Yeah. All done."

"Well, good because I wanted to ask you who we should call about the sink."

"The sink?"

He glanced over at the stainless-steel sink along the

wall. The water that filled one side nearly to the top had globs of pink buttercream floating in it.

"Just a guess, but I'm pretty sure it's clogged."

"Oh, really?" he said.

Caroline grinned before turning serious again. "Do you know which plumber your mother usually works with?"

"None, if she can help it."

"We've got to do *something*. And soon," Margie said in the tight tone of an artist under stress. "We have to have one of these cakes delivered to the community center and the other one to Lakeside Country Club by twelve-thirty."

Caroline waved away the decorator's concern with a brush of her hand. "Don't worry. We'll be fine. We've got this under control." She turned back to Logan. "At least I hope Logan does."

Though the frenzy of activity continued around them, staff members took turns sending curious glances at their temporary bosses.

Caroline gestured toward the sink and then turned back to Logan. Her wide-eyed expression of an ingenue made him fight back a grin. He would have to razz her later for pouring her act on so thick. The woman who never needed anything from anyone was offering him the chance to come to the rescue in front of the whole staff.

"I'll take a look first, and then I'll call in a professional if it's going to be too big a job."

"Sounds like a good plan to me," she said.

He still half expected Caroline to stand around, watching him and second-guessing his work. Instead, she headed to the office. Though she was probably just helping him establish a position of authority so she could leave without guilt when she found a new job, he still appreciated her vote of confidence.

He turned back to the staff, who all pretended not to be watching. "Just let me get my tools."

His tool belt was just where he'd left it in the tall cabinet inside the storage room. Good thing he'd thought to leave tools and a pair of coveralls there the other day. He'd learned the hard way that his motorcycle needed a tune-up soon.

After pulling on the coveralls, he returned with a bucket and his tools, scooting on his back under the sink. Around him, he could hear the whir of beaters, the chatter of voices and even the jingle of bells, announcing customers, but he stayed focused on the task at hand. Caroline believed he could handle the job, and there was no way he wouldn't earn that belief.

Good thing for him the job wasn't a big one: just a blob of chocolate goo turning the sink trap into a confectioner's dam. Somehow he managed to open up the trap and chisel out the blockage without being drowned by the tidal wave once it broke loose.

He had just pushed out from beneath the sink and had turned to collect the bucket filled with nasty water when he heard approaching footsteps.

"How's life in the bakery business, little brother?" Matthew asked.

"Some days are better than others." His smile probably looked forced, but he didn't care. He was frustrated that the family continued to check up on him at the bakery.

Matthew gestured toward the bucket. "I take it today is one of the worse ones?"

"It's definitely having its moments." Instead of waiting for Matthew to give some excuse about why he was there, Logan hefted the bucket and carried it toward the storage room where he would pour it down the utility sink.

Matthew followed him down the hall but paused when Caroline came out of the office.

"Oh, Matthew. I didn't know you were here." She glanced to the kitchen and then back at him. "Did you come to check up on us?"

Logan rounded the corner as fast as he could and poured the bucket into the sink. He was glad they couldn't see him because it would have been impossible to hide his grin. Leave it to Caroline Scott to lay it all on the line.

Clearly she'd caught his brother off guard because he cleared his throat a few times before he answered.

"Uh. Well, I heard you're doing your first weddings today, so I wanted to come by and…ah…see if there was anything the rest of us could do to help out."

Logan set the empty bucket inside the sink and then crossed back to stand next to Caroline. "Hey, thanks for the offer, but everything seems to be under control. We'll have these cakes off to the receptions in no time."

Logan shouldn't have let it bother him that Matthew didn't look convinced, but he did. He waited for Caroline to contradict him and to insist that they accept his brother's help. Matthew was, after all, the other firstborn overachiever in their families, the only Warren brother she would trust to do a job to her expectations.

"He's right, Matthew." At Logan's surprised glance, she grinned. "We had a problem with the sink this morning, but Logan took care of it in no time. Otherwise, everything's moving like clockwork."

Matthew took another look down the hall to the kitchen and then turned back to them. "Well, that's great. Glad to hear it. I have to pick up more cleaning supplies for Haley, anyway."

"You know she's not supposed to be working with harsh cleaners," Caroline said. "It's not good for the baby."

But Matthew only chuckled at that. "Oh, I know. Haley knows it, too. That's why she's having *me* use them instead, while she drinks lemonade and plays in the sandbox with Lizzie."

Though he laughed with the others, Logan couldn't help sneaking a peek at Caroline. Just when he thought he'd figured her out, she surprised him again. It crossed his mind to wonder why he continued to expect the worst of her, but he decided not to analyze that. He probably wouldn't like what he found if he did.

"My baby sister." Caroline smiled with pride. "I taught her well."

As soon as his brother headed out the door again, Logan turned back to her.

"You seemed awfully certain. You haven't even been back in the kitchen. How do you know I fixed the sink?"

"Didn't you?"

"Well, yeah, but—"

"But nothing. I've seen you and your brothers fix anything from a running toilet to a window-sized hole in a ceiling." She drew her eyebrows together. "Have you forgotten last Christmas when we fixed up that house for the Denton family?"

"How could I forget that? That place was a disaster when we started working."

"Then why would you wonder how I would know that you could fix a simple sink clog? If nothing else, the Warren guys are handy. I had no reason to worry."

"Thanks." But as understanding dawned, he crossed his arms. "Wait. You knew it was that simple, and you had me come in to handle it? Was it just so you could give me a chance to prove myself to the staff?"

"Not just that." As she stared down at her hands, a small smile played on her lips. "I didn't want to get *my* hands dirty."

"At least you had a good reason."

"That and I was trying to follow the suggestion from a wise group called The Beatles that we all do better with some help from our friends."

"Okay, this is going to be an odd day if you're going to start citing wisdom from *Sgt. Pepper* this early."

"Next time I'll wait until after lunch."

"Good. Now we have that settled." He cleared his throat. "Anyway, thanks."

"You're welcome."

At the loud chatter coming from the kitchen, Logan started down the hall with Caroline at his heels. No matter what they'd just told his brother, it appeared that they would be putting out fires all day at the bakery, and he could only hope it wouldn't be literal fires.

"What do you think?" Kamie gestured like a game-show hostess to the three-tier wedding cake with fresh yellow flowers on top and leafy vines trailing down its sides. "It's done."

The others, who had turned from their other activities, broke out in applause.

"Great job, ladies," Logan told her. "I'm sure the bride and groom will be impressed."

"As long as we get it and the other one to the receptions without damaging them," Margie added.

"We will," he assured them. "Those weddings—at least our part in them—will be perfect."

"Yeah, perfect," Caroline echoed.

When Logan glanced over at her, he expected her to be grinning, chuckling even. He wasn't disappointed. Mirth danced in her eyes, bringing a touch of light to their sapphire depths. But her smile changed then, becoming so warm and potent that Logan's knees nearly buckled.

He'd imagined the change; that had to be it. This wouldn't be the first time he'd misread signals from Caroline. Still, he couldn't shake the feeling. If anyone else had looked at him that way, or said some of the same things she'd said to him this morning, he would have been certain that person was flirting, but this was Caroline Scott. His instincts were off when it came to her, his tried-and-true methods for dealing with women as ineffective as a trip with all left turns.

He hadn't imagined it, he decided. She probably smiled that way with all of her friends. But if that was the case and he could expect more smiles like that in the coming weeks, he was especially glad to count himself among Caroline's friends.

Chapter Six

"Two cakes today?"

Caroline smiled at the question that came out of Amy's mouth before Caroline and Logan had made it through the door of the new room in the hospital's rehabilitation center. The reality that Logan's mother was sitting up in a wheelchair made her smile even more.

She didn't even feel guilty for skipping the chance to spend another afternoon job-searching on her mother's interminably slow Internet connection. Hadn't somebody outlawed dial-up by now? Anyway, the chance to see Mrs. Warren out of bed was worth any job leads she missed.

"Well, somebody's having a good day," Caroline said.

Amy looked great, too. She wore a fluffy bathrobe over her hospital gown, and her silver hair, though not styled the way she usually wore it, was clean and combed.

This room was bigger than the last one, with four beds instead of two, all for stroke patients or those recovering from other types of brain injuries. A woman in her late fifties slept in the bed nearest the door, but the three remaining beds, including Amy's, were empty.

"Hi, beautiful." Logan kissed his mother's cheek and then rubbed the side of his forefinger along her jawline. Lowering his hand, Logan helped Amy adjust the blanket in her lap so that her weaker left hand rested on top of the cloth.

Caroline swallowed, the intimate scene making her chest feel tight. Logan was such an attentive son, visiting his mother every day on his lunch hour and many evenings after work, as well. His tireless care for his mother—that had to be what had touched Caroline so deeply. So why did she suddenly wonder what it would feel like if hers were the cheek he'd kissed, if her face was the one he'd touched?

"Two?"

Caroline was grateful Amy had repeated the question, giving her the chance to avoid her own questions. They were becoming tougher and tougher to answer.

"Technically, it's three if you count the simple two-layer that Kamie finished up late this afternoon for tonight's ceremony at the assisted living center," Logan told her. "Young love. Ain't it grand?"

"I thought it was sweet," Caroline said, frowning at him. "Two widowed seniors in their eighties have found love again. You should have seen how cute they were when I went to the center to take their order."

Surprised by her own words, Caroline stared at the floor. When had she become a romantic, anyway? Some women swooned over things like baby's breath, cathedral-length trains and proposals in horse-drawn carriages. She'd never been one of those women. So she was as mystified by her comment as she had been over becoming misty-eyed when that sweet senior lady had described the pillbox hat she'd ordered for her wedding.

When she finally looked up again, Logan was grinning at her. Like always, he'd just been trying to get a rise out of his mother and her. But as his gaze moved to his mother again, that smile vanished. Though he blinked a few times, his eyes remained suspiciously shiny. Instead of the warning frown that Amy usually would have given her son after one of his facetious comments, she wore a blank expression, as if she'd missed the joke.

Caroline knew what he had to be thinking. The neurologist had warned them that some stroke patients lost their sense of humor or had other personality changes after a stroke. That couldn't happen to Mrs. Warren, not the woman who served laughter in daily doses in her home. The loss of Amy's sweet personality would be like a death of another kind.

Caroline couldn't help glancing at Logan again. She longed to gather her friend in her arms and tell him not to worry, but she couldn't offer that kind of assurance. No one could. Mrs. Warren was improving every day, but the doctors warned there would be limits on how far her recovery would go.

"Three is good. June now," Amy said, returning to the earlier subject as she often did lately. She had a hard time following quick transitions in a conversation.

Logan cleared his throat, but he managed to smile at his mother. "Yes, it is June, Mom."

"Biggest…wedding month," she continued.

"We're doing fine," he assured her. "Getting out

orders on time. Even bringing in new orders for fall weddings."

"You should see it, Mrs. Warren. Ranger Logan's doing a great job."

His gaze flicked to Caroline, and he gave her a look she couldn't read before he turned back to his mother. She hoped he didn't think she was trying to remind his mother that he was ill-suited for work at the bakery, because she hadn't meant that at all.

"We would be doing even better if you were back again," Logan told her.

"Might not go back."

"Of course you will." Pulling a chair up next to Amy's wheelchair, Logan laid his fingers over her curled left hand. "You just have a few things to do here first."

"So what did you do in physical therapy today?" Caroline asked, drawing another chair over and taking a seat. She glanced at Amy's bed, which was freshly made up with hospital corners. "Did they have you up walking?"

"Hard," Amy said.

"Oh, I know it must be. But you did walk, right?"

"In the hall."

"Mom, that's great," Logan said, leaning over to press his cheek to hers. "I can't believe you didn't tell us that good news right away. You're making amazing progress."

Amy only shrugged.

Logan glanced away, his Adam's apple shifting as he swallowed a few times before looking back.

A hospital employee brought a dining tray in then, giving them the chance to let the subject drop. Caroline didn't know what to say, anyway. She doubted Logan would admit it, but his mother's progress had been slower than any of them had hoped.

Mrs. Warren's attitude worried her, as well. Caroline had always admired her for being so relentlessly positive, even after her husband left. Now she didn't have a positive thing to say. She no longer seemed to have hope.

Logan continued to praise his mother's small accomplishments as she fed herself with her good hand, and when she didn't notice the drip of chicken broth that landed on her chin, he dabbed it with a napkin.

"There you go. Good as new."

But after he said it, his gaze darted to Caroline, his expression as stark and hopeless as his mother's words had been. They couldn't call anything about Amy's appearance or her new pessimistic attitude *as good as new*.

"Well, look who's already entertaining a crowd," Dylan called from the doorway, where he stood with Jenna. Still dressed in her navy flight attendant uniform, Jenna waved as she entered the room.

"Yeah, it's quite a party in here."

Logan turned to the window and pinched the bridge of his nose as he spoke, but when he turned back again, he had control over his emotions. Caroline and Jenna exchanged a knowing look, but in true guy form, Dylan pretended not to notice his brother's emotional moment.

Dylan sauntered across the room and leaned over to hug his mother.

"Two cakes today," Amy told him as soon as he released her.

Logan shook his head as he stood and moved his

mother's tray table off to the side. Instead of sitting again, he gestured for Dylan to take his place. "No, Mom. Three. Remember?"

"Three," she said, nodding her head.

"That's good news, Mom." Dylan lowered into the seat next to her, taking her hand. "It is June, after all."

"June," she repeated.

As Dylan sat, he shot a glance at his younger brother and cleared his throat. "Since you two have already had a nice visit with Mom, why don't you get out of here and give us a turn."

Moving closer to her fiancé, Jenna rested a hand on Dylan's shoulder and used the other hand to wave toward the door. "Yeah, you guys. Hit the road."

"Isn't it bad enough that I'm twenty-four years old and my big brothers are still telling me what to do?" Logan stacked two smaller bowls on his mother's plate and put the cover on her dinner tray. "Now I have to let my *future* sister-in-law push me around, too?"

Though he protested, Logan couldn't seem to get out of the room fast enough. They said their goodbyes, and he hurried out of the room, leaving Caroline to follow gamely behind him. Once they'd passed through the heavy metal doors marking the exit from the rehabilitation department, Logan sagged against the wall. He squeezed his eyes shut and shoved his hands back through his hair.

"That was a rough one." Caroline sighed and leaned on the wall.

"Ya think?" But Logan's lips lifted in a sad smile as he opened his eyes.

He waited, as if he expected her to say more, but

when she didn't, he shook his head. "I thought it would get easier seeing her like this."

His voice was so thick with emotion that Caroline had to clasp her hands together to keep from grabbing him in a hug that would only embarrass him. He probably hated feeling vulnerable as much as she did.

"But she's doing so much better, Logan. You heard her. She was walking today. Walking! Three weeks ago you weren't even sure she would survive the stroke, and now she's sitting up and feeding herself and—"

Logan held up a hand to stop her speech. "And walking. I know." He shook his head. "I don't know what I expected. Maybe that she would recover almost like Lazarus or something, and then we could all go out to lunch."

She smiled at him because she realized that though he had phrased it in a funny way, he really had hoped, realistically or not, for a speedy miracle. "You told me yourself that her progress would be slow. Weren't you listening to yourself?"

He lifted a shoulder and let it fall. "I feel rotten for not being more appreciative. Not counting our blessings for how far Mom's come. But it's just that she's not… you know…she's not…"

"Herself?" Caroline supplied as her gaze met his. "I know what you mean."

"She doesn't get the jokes. She doesn't laugh." He swallowed visibly. "You know what the doctors said."

"About personality changes? You don't know that that's going to happen. Not every stroke patient experiences those kinds of changes."

He crossed his arms as if for self-protection and stared at the shiny linoleum of the hallway floor.

"What if it does happen? What if Mom's never the same person again?"

"She'll still be your mother."

Caroline didn't mean for her words to come out so harshly, so she braced herself for whatever Logan would say next. Had she overstepped her boundaries? She might love Mrs. Warren, but this was Logan's mother. What kind of friend was she, anyway? He'd opened his feelings to her, and she'd stomped all over them.

"You're right."

She wasn't sure she'd heard him correctly, so she looked at him, finding him staring back at her.

"Thanks. I needed to hear it." Logan pushed his fingers through his hair again as he settled back against the wall, but he didn't seem as frustrated as he had earlier.

"The doctors also told you it's going to be months before we know what the extent of your mom's recovery is going to be. You'll just have to be patient."

When Logan turned his wide-eyed expression on her, she chuckled. "I know. I know. That's tough advice to take from someone like me."

"You can say that again."

She grinned. "That's tough advice to—"

"Okay. Once was enough." Gesturing for her to follow him, Logan started down the hall, but he glanced back over his shoulder at her. "Thanks again."

She caught up to walk beside him. "You're welcome."

Logan's step appeared lighter as they walked out of the hospital, and Caroline was glad for him. Unfortunately, her heart felt heavier. As sad as she'd been during the visit with Mrs. Warren, especially watching her son's reaction to it, the time had been eye-opening for her. Before she'd been asking *when* Mrs. Warren would return to her bakery, but now she had to wonder *if* that would ever happen.

Did Logan even see it yet? She could only imagine how painful it would be for him to realize that his mother had survived the stroke only to lose her personality in the process. Was he ready to acknowledge that there might be other limitations to her recovery? That she might never return to work?

Caroline already knew the answer to that. Logan worked every day with the intensity of a man with hope and a deadline. How could she shatter his belief by telling him she didn't trust that his mother would even return? But she had to. Though Caroline would only be at the bakery a short while, Logan and his brothers would be left with a business to run. They had to decide what to do with Amy's Elite Treats if its namesake never returned to bake again.

"You finally set a date!"

Logan hadn't even reached Trina Scott's backyard, but he would have heard her exclamation from as far away as his downtown apartment. He unlocked the gate and found his family and the Scotts as they often were, in a crushing group hug.

Opposite that group, a picnic table had been covered with a vinyl tablecloth, and platters of food were spread over the length of it. Delicious smells seeped from the grill, making his stomach growl.

He was glad he'd let Mrs. Scott talk him into coming this time instead of excusing himself for another "date" at the park. Even if his mother couldn't be with them today, she would still want the two families to enjoy time together, especially on a day when they could celebrate Dylan and Jenna's good news.

He scanned the faces of the friends and relatives around the yard, not even realizing he'd been searching for Caroline until he felt a thud of disappointment when she wasn't there. Where was she? If she was staying at her mother's house, how had she managed to avoid attending the cookout?

Just like each morning at the bakery, he couldn't help watching for her and waiting for that undeniable jolt as soon as she came into view. This wasn't good. No, not good.

Lizzie was the first to unravel from the knot of people. "Look. Uncle Logan's here." She ran over, and in a practiced move, propelled herself into his arms. He shifted her to his hip.

"What's up, kiddo?"

"Did you hear about the wedding?" Her eyes were as big as quarters as she spoke.

"I did just now. That's great."

She straightened in his arms. "I get to be a flower girl again. Two times."

"Hey, that's a big deal."

Lizzie bubbled with excitement. "None of my friends have been a flower girl two times."

The child prattled on about a new dress and new shoes and whatever else little girls get all hyped up about in weddings, but Logan barely heard any of it. He was too busy trying to shake away the image of his niece in a third flower girl dress, with a surprising pair as the bride and groom.

Where had that thought come from, and what could

he do to make it stop? He wasn't the marrying kind. He'd always known that. He didn't even date anyone long-term. He would not be like his father, not if he could help it. So what was he going to do about Caroline Scott and the way she made him want to forget who he was?

This wasn't good. Not good at all.

"Aren't you going to congratulate me, brother?"

Logan started, surprised to see that Dylan had made it all the way over to him before he'd noticed. Great. Now he was becoming a virtual Walter Mitty, daydreaming about weddings and the most unlikely bride he could ever imagine.

"Sure I am." Lowering Lizzie to the ground, he grasped his brother in a bear hug. "But did you really set a date, or are you just playing a cruel joke on poor Mrs. Scott?"

"I'd never do a thing like that to my future mother-in-law, but we did scare her by telling her we were just going to have a civil ceremony on Wednesday."

"Now that *was* cruel."

"I thought she was going to blow a gasket before we told her we were only kidding."

Logan spotted Trina across the lawn, laughing as she rubbed her hand over Haley's rounded belly, so he guessed she'd survived the joke. "So when's the real date?"

"July twelfth." Dylan beamed. "We just confirmed it with Reverend Boggs."

"That's just over a month. Are you going to be able to pull it off?"

"It was the only date open at our church until the end of August."

Logan lifted a brow. "After stalling all this time, you're in a hurry now?"

"You kidding? I'd marry her tomorrow if she'd let me. I've been waiting my whole life to be Jenna's husband." Dylan patted his younger brother on the shoulder. "I hope someday you find someone you can care about as much as I love her."

"I'm happy for you." Logan patted Dylan's arm, refusing to let his thoughts travel to dangerous places again. No more Walter Mitty adventures for him today. "Wait. When did Haley say she was due?"

"August first."

"You guys are cutting it close."

Approaching them, Jenna took Dylan's arm. "We are, but Matthew and Haley agree with Mom that we should go ahead with the wedding. It will give your mother something else to look forward to. When we told her, she said that it was, and I quote, 'good.'"

"Of course she would say that," Logan told them. "She wants to make sure her matchmaking targets get hitched. And mark my words, the ink will still be drying on your marriage license before she'll be bugging you about adding to her brood of grandchildren."

"Whoa. Don't even go there yet." Dylan wrapped his arm around his fiancée's shoulder and turned to kiss her cheek. "But someday Jenna and I will have some beautiful babies."

"You kidding?" Logan said with a grin. "You'll have enough of them to field your own baseball team before your tenth anniversary."

"Or at least a beach volleyball team," Matthew chimed as he joined them.

Laughter filled the backyard as Haley and Trina

stepped over to complete the group. Logan joined in, but he couldn't resist looking past the others, still searching for the missing Scott sister. "Has Caroline heard the news?"

"No, we just told the others—" Jenna stopped and gave him a sharp look. "You're not worried she'll be upset, are you? She's always seemed to be happy for us before. You don't think...?"

Logan was shaking his head before she could finish. "No. She'll be thrilled for you guys though she'll be bummed she missed your announcement...wherever she is."

He tried to sound nonchalant as he added that last part, inserting a mini fishing expedition while hoping not to get caught himself. The last thing he wanted was to make anyone suspect that he was overly interested in the whereabouts of one Caroline Scott. Or that he had any interest in her at all besides as coworker and friend. He didn't. That was his story, and he was sticking to it.

Jenna looked relieved. "That's good because I can't wait to ask her—"

"Look at you guys," Caroline called out as she crossed the yard, carrying two plastic shopping bags. "I was gone only five minutes. I even leave the party to go buy the buns *somebody else* forgot, and I come back to find you all talking about me."

"We weren't— I was just—" Logan stopped and gestured for Jenna to take over for him.

Jenna gave him a funny look before turning back to her sister. "Logan was just wondering why you weren't here for our big announcement."

"What big announcement?" Caroline looked back

and forth between her sister and Dylan and then grinned as she held up her cell phone. "I heard. You think I could have one of these, and Mom wouldn't be able to reach me within seconds when she had good news?"

"Thanks, Mom." Jenna rolled her eyes.

Trina was unapologetic. "You made me wait months for this, so I plan to enjoy every minute of it."

"Anyway," Jenna tried again, turning to Caroline, "since you already know about the date, I wanted to ask you to be my maid of honor."

Instead of answering, Caroline shot a glance at Haley.

"Me?" Haley said. "There's no way I'm going to try to squeeze all of this into a bridesmaid's dress less than three weeks before my due date." She indicated her expanding belly.

Jenna looked from one sister to the other. "You see, I didn't even have to choose between you two."

"Then I'd love to do it," Caroline said with a smile.

"And I don't have to choose, either, because Matthew volunteered to plan the wedding music instead," Dylan said. "So I guess that leaves you, buddy. Are you in?"

"You know how much I *love* weddings." But after getting the laugh, Logan nodded. "But sure. I'll do it."

"Sure you don't have a date that day?" Matthew wanted to know.

"If I do, I can reschedule." Logan frowned at his oldest brother, but when he glanced sidelong at Caroline, he caught her watching him. Was it wrong of him to wish that she would be a little jealous of his nonexistent dates? Wrong and dangerous, he decided. Dangerous to him.

"I just know Amy will be well enough to attend,

and it's going to be perfect." Trina folded her arms, the satisfied grin of a successful matchmaker on her lips.

"It will as long as you ask Mr. Kellam to be your escort," Haley chimed.

"Don't you start." Trina probably would have continued her lecture, but something caught her attention, making her turn toward the grill. "Well, there go the brats."

Matthew and Dylan rushed over to the smoking grill, but it was too late to save the charred meat, so another trip to the store for replacements would be required.

Why did Logan have the feeling that the cookout that had just gone up in flames might be a better reflection of what the wedding might be like than the perfection Mrs. Scott had predicted? At least for him.

He wanted to say he could do this. He had survived being in Matthew and Haley's wedding last summer, but this time was different. This time he would be escorting Caroline. Wasn't it hard enough working every day with her and pretending not to notice how beautiful, how clever and how compassionate she was?

How could he escort her down that aisle and stand near her, just a breath away from the altar, and not get some crazy ideas in his head about a more unlikely bride and groom?

Chapter Seven

Caroline expected only the dull glow of a single safety light when she unlocked the bakery's back door, so the brightness coming from inside startled her. She was already making a mental note to remind staff about turning off lights when a sound came from the office, signaling that she wasn't alone.

Remembering that first day when Logan had mistakenly thought the front door had been left unlocked, she stiffened. Had someone really forgotten today? Her pulse quickened, and her senses clicked into high alert. This part of Markston might have been a low-crime area, but Caroline reasoned that every neighborhood had that same spotless record until the break-ins, carjackings and murders began.

Scanning the hall for a weapon she could use, if necessary, she caught sight of Logan's riding boots beneath the coat rack. His leather jacket hung from a hook just above them. Her breath caught. She should be relieved that Logan was in that office instead of some prowler intent on raiding the safe, but her pulse didn't slow in the comfort of that knowledge. If anything, it beat even faster.

Just in case she was wrong about the visitor's identity, Caroline grabbed a wooden hanger and crept down the hall toward the lighted room. Feeling ridiculous, she tiptoed to the half-open door and peeked inside.

Logan sat at the desk, surrounded by a pile of open books. His shoulders were bent, and his head was bowed. Was he praying? She'd pictured Logan Warren a few different ways these last few weeks—chopping wood with his arm muscles flexing, riding his motorcycle with his leather jacket whipping in the wind, even on dinner dates with every single woman in town besides her. But praying? She hadn't expected that.

Instead of looking away and giving him privacy, Caroline couldn't help continuing to watch him. She supposed it shouldn't surprise her to learn that Logan was a praying man. She'd learned in the past few weeks that the boy she'd thought she knew didn't resemble the man she was coming to know at all. Instead of being surprised to find Logan praying, she should be wondering why she'd spent so little time in prayer lately.

Caroline had just decided to slip out unnoticed when Logan lifted his head. His shoulders stiffened as if he could sense someone else's presence, and he turned his head to look at the doorway.

"What—" He jumped up from his seat and then turned back to shuffle the materials on the desk.

"Sorry. I didn't mean to startle you." She moved just inside the door, setting the hanger on top of the bookshelf.

"Uh, you didn't," he said, though she obviously had.

"That's good." With her gaze, she followed his jerky movements as he tried to hide whatever he'd been reading. That he didn't want her to see it only made her more curious. "I didn't see your bike when I pulled in."

"Parked it on the street. I, uh, didn't expect to see you here tonight. Why *are* you here?"

"You know me, the workaholic." Caroline shifted. She didn't want to admit she didn't have anything better to do on a Saturday night. "The only way you can keep me out of the workplace is to bar the windows and doors." She cleared her throat. "Or downsize my job."

"Tried to do that here. It didn't work out so well."

He kept messing with what appeared to be a stack of magazines until he had them in a pile at the edge of the desk, but when he turned to face her, the copies on top of the stack slid to the floor.

Caroline took a few steps forward and bent to stare down at the magazine covers. Where she might have expected *National Geographic* or *The Outdoorsman,* she was surprised to see *American Cake Decorating* and *Indiana Bride.*

With a frustrated breath, Logan bent to grab the magazines, stacking them back on the desk with a whole collection of similar titles.

"Reading up for your stint as the best man?"

Logan turned back to her, crossing his arms over his chest. "That's the best you've got?"

"Well, I was going to ask you about your take on the cathedral-length-train-versus-chapel-length controversy. Or maybe get your opinion on Miss Manners's reception seating chart for step-siblings."

Logan shot his hands into the air as if she held him at gunpoint. "Stop. Stop. I can't take it anymore."

"Come on," Caroline said, chuckling. "I haven't even gotten to the nosegays or boutonnieres yet."

"Nose whats?"

She waved away his question. "Never mind. Okay, I'll bite. What are you doing in your mother's office on a Saturday night, surrounded by bridal and cake magazines? Giving up being Ranger Logan in favor of a new career as Logan the wedding planner?"

"I'll pass." He glanced at the desk and shrugged. "Since I'm working here, I figured I should learn something about the wedding business."

"I think that's a great idea."

He tilted his head, his gaze narrowing.

"I'm serious," she told him. "Your mom will be proud, too, when she finds out all you've done for her business."

Now didn't seem like time to tell him she suspected that Mrs. Warren would never return to the shop. Somehow she doubted the time would ever be right.

"Thanks," he said finally.

She noticed that he shifted more uncomfortably because of her praise than he ever had from one of her wisecracks.

"I probably would have known a lot more about the wedding business before if I'd been paying attention." He brushed his hand over the slick cover of one of the magazines. "Mom made the cakes, and Matthew planned all the wedding music at our church. I could have gleaned a few things from them."

"So, you're like everyone else. You learn on a need-to-know basis."

"I guess. Well, do you want to look at these with me?" As he waited for her answer, he gathered the magazines and motioned with a turn of his head for her to come with him.

"Why are we going out here?" she asked as she followed him through the kitchen and out into the dining area.

"A couple of reasons. First, don't you agree the light is better out here?"

Caroline lifted her head to stare at the series of hanging lamps that offered little more than ambience. A lot of light wasn't necessary, though, because daylight usually poured in from the windows, and even now glare from the streetlamps filled the room.

"I also get claustrophobic in that office," he said. "It's too cramped in there."

"Yeah, it is." *You have no idea.* But then every room seemed uncomfortably close when she and Logan were in it together. She decided not to share that bit of information.

He used his thumb to indicate the front of the shop. "But mostly, I came out here because I ordered a pizza, and the guy prefers to deliver to the front door after dark."

"You often order here in the evenings?" It was a sneaky way of asking how often he'd been working there at night, but she couldn't help being curious. Not about his overtime work, either. If he was at the bakery, he couldn't have been on all those dates she'd imagined.

"Sometimes." He was watching the street, waiting for the driver, but he glanced back. "The people at The Pie know my phone voice now, so they ask if I want my regular."

"What's your regular?"

"Not deluxe the way you and Matthew like to order it. Just pepperoni and black olives."

Caroline covered her eyes with her hand. "Oh, I'll never forget that night when our moms tried to push Matthew and me together at The Pie. It was so embarrassing. Mom had this crazy idea Matthew and I were perfect for each other just because we liked the same stuff on our pizza."

"Well, you *did* have an awful lot in common." The side of his mouth lifted. "Same goals. Same books. Same—"

"But could you ever picture Matthew with anyone but Haley? Me especially. That would have been like marrying myself."

"No, I couldn't."

She had been chuckling as she stared out the window, but Logan's words and his reflection in the glass quieted her. When she would have expected him to be smiling, his jaw was flexed instead. By the time that she could turn to take a better look at him, the expression was gone. Still, she was sure she hadn't mistaken it. He might not have been able to imagine her with his oldest brother, but something else was bothering him.

She was trying to come up with some pithy comment to lighten the mood when a car pulled to the curb, a lighted sign for The Pie on its roof.

Logan reached in the back pocket of his well-worn jeans and pulled out his wallet. "I was going to offer to share, but since it's not deluxe, I guess I'll get the whole pizza to myself."

"I'm not picky," she was quick to say. "I like all kinds of pizza."

As soon as he nodded and crossed to open the door

for the delivery guy, who carried both pizza and a two-liter bottle of soda, Caroline's hands started to sweat. It was just pizza, she reminded herself. That and the chance to look at a bunch of bridal magazines. But the reality struck her that it was the closest thing she'd had to a date in years.

Logan set the pizza box on the floor beside him and patted his full stomach as Caroline finished her last slice of pizza and wiped her fingertips on a napkin.

"You didn't say you were starved." He was grinning as he said it. They'd split the pizza right down the middle, and she'd polished off her half almost as quickly as he had. She was such a refreshing change from the women he'd known—women who ate like birds as if that was supposed to impress him or something.

"You didn't ask."

"Next time I'll ask." He took a drink from one of the foam coffee cups they'd used for the soda and then reached for the magazines stacked on the floor next to him. "And maybe order two pizzas."

Next time. That sounded a little too good to him. Not only was he having more fun on this nondate than he'd had on any date in years, now he also was trying to set up a second nondate. He never had second dates.

Logan was relieved he'd had the good sense to bring her out into the dining area instead of spending more time alone with her in that postage-sized office. In there, he could smell jasmine on her hair every time she moved, and she was close enough to touch no matter where they stood or sat. The dining area offered not only the space for him to keep a safer distance, but it provided a chaperone of sorts, as they were under the watchful eyes of the streetlamps and passing cars.

"You do that and I'll never fit in my maid-of-honor dress unless Jenna picks a dome tent."

He wanted to tell her she would still look amazing, even dressed in a tent, but that would have only made the dining area feel as small as the office had. As Caroline grabbed a cake magazine and started flipping through the pages, he couldn't help watching her.

"So how do you feel about the upcoming wedding?"

She shrugged, not looking up from the pages. "It's great, I guess. I hope they're not rushing the wedding just to give your mom something to look forward to."

"You don't think they're doing that, do you?"

"Not really. But you know how my mother can get what she wants out of my sisters."

"But not you," he said with a laugh.

Leaning forward and resting her forearms on the table, she smiled. "No, not me."

Her smile was so sweet and potent that a weaker guy would have been tempted to be drawn in by it. He had to glance out the window to refocus his thoughts and keep from becoming that guy.

"I wouldn't worry about Jenna getting pushed into anything, either," he told her. "Look at how long she made Dylan wait for her. Stubbornness is definitely a Scott family trait."

"You're right about that."

"At least with them planning the wedding right now, you'll be around to help Jenna with the details instead of just flying in from Chicago at the last minute."

Logan wondered if it could be any more obvious that

he was fishing for information about her job search. She would surely jump to the conclusion that he was counting down the days until she left. She would be wrong.

"For a while, I guess," she said vaguely. But then she leaned forward as if to offer some solid information. "Are your bosses nagging you yet about getting back to your Ranger Logan job?"

He frowned, but only partially because she hadn't given him a single clue about her plans. It was time he cleared up her confusion about him.

"You know that's a nickname, don't you?" Her confused expression didn't surprise him. "The Ranger Logan thing. It's just what my brothers call me."

"I don't understand. You don't work at Boyton County State Park?"

"No, that part's right. It's the title that's wrong. I'm a state park biologist—or wildlife specialist—for the Indiana Department of Natural Resources."

"But I thought—" She stopped herself, clearly at a loss for words.

"Matthew and Dylan just thought Ranger Logan sounded a lot more fun than Park Biologist Logan or Wildlife Specialist Logan. Those names don't have the same ring to them."

Caroline's hand went to her mouth. "I'm so sorry. I never meant to offend you."

"Now don't get me wrong." He shook his head. "I believe that park ranger is an honorable job. It's just not *my* job."

She must have recovered her embarrassment because she leaned back in her chair and crossed her arms. "So how does one end up working as a park biologist?"

"I started with a forestry degree from Purdue, and a

minor in wildlife sciences." He couldn't help grinning as he warmed to the subject. "It's great. Instead of sitting behind some desk all day, I get to be outside, overseeing food-plot plantings, conducting wildlife population surveys and managing the walleye stocking program."

"Sounds interesting."

"It's the best."

She shook her head. "And you think you know someone."

Logan didn't look back at her, but he could feel her gaze on him.

"Do you miss it?" she asked.

"Well, sure, but here is where I need to be right now. Mom needs me."

"You gave up a lot to be here."

Strange, she'd said things like this before, but for the first time, he believed she really meant her praise. He couldn't help feeling flattered by it. "Not as much as my mother has always given up for me. Anyway, it'll only be for a while."

She nodded though her eyes were filled with doubt. He'd been having some doubts himself, but he couldn't say them aloud. That would be admitting he was giving up, and there was no way he would give up on his mother's recovery.

"In the meantime, I think it's great how hard you're working to learn your mother's business."

"I've definitely learned that violet is the new pink in bridesmaids' dresses." He flipped to an article with a headline saying that exact thing and turned the magazine around so she could take a look. "And that the majority of wedding cakes are made with fondant now though my mother still prefers to work with buttercream frosting."

He pointed to the cover of a second magazine where a bridal shower cake was shaped to look like a blue purse, complete with dark blue stitching accents.

"Those are both very important wedding business tidbits."

"I'm going to learn a lot more here." Pulling out a community education brochure he'd stacked on the bottom of the pile of magazines, he pointed to a class description.

"Cake decorating? Are you thinking about taking that class?"

"Depends on whether you'll make fun of me about it."

Caroline folded her arms and frowned at him. "Are you telling me that you would let my opinion determine whether you take a class you're interested in?"

He shook his head, grinning. "Never said that. I just figured if you're going to make fun of me about it, I won't *tell you* I'm already registered for that class. I'm not trying to become a decorator or anything. I just want to have a basic knowledge of the lingo and the skills."

"Well, good, then." She smiled back at him. "You would have disappointed me if you caved in so easily."

"Wouldn't want to do that."

As soon as he said it, Logan realized how true it was. He didn't want to disappoint Caroline any more than he wanted to let down his mother. That it mattered so much to him what she thought was just another signal that he needed to put some space between them. Otherwise, he might be tempted to care about more than her opinions.

He couldn't risk becoming involved with her unless he wanted to find out if he was really like his father and take a chance at hurting her. Ignorance was bliss, and he needed to embrace it.

For a few minutes, they sat across from each other, both flipping through magazine articles without the need for conversation. He glanced up when Caroline cleared her throat.

"I don't know what you'll think about this, but would you mind if I took that class with you?"

"Do you really want to?"

"I mean, I don't even know if I can still register, but..."

Her words fell away as she looked to him, waiting for some kind of response. She probably thought he was hesitating because he was worried that she was looking for another way to run the show at the bakery. How could he tell her he was torn between wanting to stay as far away from her as possible and finding any excuse to be near her?

"It sounds like great idea to me," he said finally.

A chill scrambled up his spine as he anticipated studying with her. He needed to make more excuses to spend time *away* from her, not *near* her.

Battling his attraction to her felt like swimming upstream in river rapids, and he was tired, but, worse than that, part of him was tempted to turn and swim with the current right to a woman who might not even want him.

Chapter Eight

"Are you sure they're supposed to look like this?"

Caroline started at the sound of Logan's voice, but she still managed to keep the rosette she'd been forming close to the same size as its sister flowers on the wax paper in front of her. It was tough enough concentrating with him sitting right next to her without him interrupting her all the time.

"What's wrong now?"

She expected to see a splat of frosting on his sheet of wax paper like the mess Logan had made after he'd first tried out the pastry bag, but she what she found shocked her. Three perfect rows of rosettes lined one side of the paper and scallop edging with uniform peaks decorated the other side.

"All those wildlife surveys had to teach me something," he said with a chuckle.

"It looks like they did, but obviously creating five-year business plans didn't help me out at all."

His pastry bag in his hand, Logan took a step toward her and bent to get a better look at her work that suddenly appeared sloppier than she'd first thought.

"Gives you a lot more respect for what Margie and Kamie do, doesn't it?" he said.

She studied her work again, frowning. "That bad, huh? And I thought I was helping *you* out so much by coming to work in the bakery. You don't need my help at all. Didn't even in the beginning."

"Are you kidding? I wouldn't have survived that first day without your help. But I'll never admit I said that, even under torture, so don't bother telling my brothers."

"Thanks, and I'll remember it's our secret." She grinned at both the image of Logan braving torture and his confession about needing her help. She appreciated knowing she was needed somewhere.

"Don't worry. With a little practice, we'll both get good at this." He indicated the rosettes in front of him.

"If you get better, you'll be on the cover of *American Cake Decorating.*"

"Now I wouldn't go that far," he said, though he seemed pleased by her praise.

Caroline went back to squeezing her pastry bag, carefully shifting her wrist so she could form the pink petals of the rosette. It was the best one she'd made so far. Maybe Logan was right about practice.

She was glad they'd signed up for this class together, even if she'd had to invite herself to join him. She enjoyed spending time with Logan. Was that a crime? And if she'd happened to join him a few times this week when he was working late at the bakery, that wasn't some telling statement, either.

He was one of the few people their age she knew in Markston, besides their siblings, and she was tired of feeling like a fifth wheel with the two couples. With Logan, she just laughed and had fun. There was something to be said for that.

Glancing back over to him, she found him bent over his practice sheet, concentrating as he used his pastry bag to form another scalloped edge.

"Did you let the decorators know we were taking this class?" she asked as she watched him.

His wrist shifted, messing up his masterpiece, but he only looked over, amused. "No. Why? Did you tell them?"

"Not me. I figured that was up to you."

"Oh. Thanks." He started at the top again, tracing a smooth line of peaks and valleys. "I haven't told anyone yet. Not my mom. Especially not my brothers. They would have a heyday with it."

"If they're not proud of you for being this proactive over your work with the bakery, then they're wrong."

She didn't realize how forcefully she'd spoken until their instructor, who was moving about the room and giving suggestions, looked at her in surprise. She sensed that Logan was watching her, too, though she couldn't bring herself to look at him to know for sure. How could she explain to him why she'd placed herself squarely in his corner when she didn't know the answer herself?

"Thanks." He cleared his throat. "Can you believe there are only two more Saturdays, and we'll have survived June madness?"

"That's amazing," she said, though she found she wasn't looking forward to the end of June with as much enthusiasm as she had at first. It felt more like a deadline now than a goal.

For a few minutes, neither spoke as they focused on

their practice sheets, but when Caroline glanced up, she caught Logan watching her work. At least she thought it was her work. Or was he just watching her?

"Doing a good job," he said but quickly looked away.

"Hey, I have an idea," she said to fill the awkward moment. "You could just keep quiet about this class until the week of Dylan and Jenna's wedding, and then you could be the one to decorate their cake."

He laughed out loud at that. "Pretty ambitious, don't you think?"

"You could do it."

As soon as she said it, Caroline realized how true her words were. Logan could do anything he wanted. That wasn't something that had changed since she'd returned to Markston, either. He'd always been so much more than the funny guy everyone knew so well. Intelligent. Capable. Too intuitive for his own good. She'd just been like the others in failing to notice his many qualities.

"Maybe…but I'll be too busy with all of my amazing best man duties to have time to use my *delicious* cake-decorating skills, as well."

"Fine then. I'll let you off the hook."

"Thanks."

When he grinned at her, she smiled back, but then he suddenly leaned toward her, his gaze connecting with hers, and she could only sit frozen, waiting. Was he really going to kiss her right there in front of a whole class of future cake decorators?

But Logan only brushed his thumb across her cheek, coming away with a clump of icing. She blinked as he pulled his hand back, leaving a tingling place at the side of her mouth where his calloused skin had touched her.

"You had this," he said, showing her the small glob in his palm.

"Oh" was all she could say though she sounded like an idiot. What had she been thinking, anyway? When she jumped to a wrong conclusion, she took a flying leap. But this was worse than that. More than mistaking his plan to kiss her, she'd wanted him to do it and had been disappointed when he hadn't.

"Thank you," she finally managed. "I remember on our family trip to Gatlinburg, Matthew and I had the job of scrubbing faces for you and Haley. Now that was a big job."

"I guess I should thank you, then."

Hearing annoyance in his voice, she slid a glance his way, but he was staring at the front of the class. Their instructor stood near the whiteboard, demonstrating another skill, using a smaller decorating tip.

"With practice, all of you will become skilled at making rosettes, and creating scalloped edges will be as automatic to you as driving," the woman told them. "But it is also going to be equally important that you develop a steady hand for piping designs and for writing."

Caroline followed the instructions, but she couldn't help thinking of a different hand than those with which she worked. This particular hand was close enough to touch if she decided to stretch.

She straightened in her seat as she switched the tip on her pastry bag. What was happening to her? Could she really be developing feelings for Logan Warren? That couldn't be possible, could it? What happened to him being too young, too unambitious…too everything?

Of course she didn't have feelings for Logan. They were just friends. Anyway, did she have no more sense of self-preservation than to even consider becoming involved with a ladies' man?

Caroline pushed away the thoughts that were getting out of hand. She'd gone from imagining that Logan wanted to kiss her to creating other ideas that were equally unfathomable. She could think of only one reason this might be happening. She hadn't been kissed in so long that her romantic instincts had gone into a coma. They'd picked an unfortunate moment to awaken.

Now she had to sing those faulty instincts a lullaby before she did something really unwise like letting Logan know about the crazy things she was feeling. Or worse yet, asking him to kiss her.

Logan followed Caroline out the door and down the steps from the old bank that had been transformed into the Markston Community Education building. From around the corner, he could see the glow from the streetlamps that lined Washington Street.

"Hey, what's the hurry?" he said when he caught up with her on the sidewalk that led to the lighted parking area.

"Oh…I wasn't," she began, but then she slowed her pace. "I was just thinking about getting home."

"Did you forget that I drove?"

"Right."

He was glad he'd insisted on driving this time and had brought his old Ford pickup that he usually only drove when it wasn't motorcycle weather. Otherwise, Caroline already would have taken off like the rest of their classmates had.

She'd been acting strangely since he'd wiped the

frosting off her face, so he wanted to get the chance to apologize. If she'd known that he'd really been considering kissing that frosting right off her cheek, she might have been relieved he'd only cleaned her up instead.

"Hey, sorry about that thing with the frosting. I just didn't want you to be embarrassed later when you realized you had it on your face."

"I appreciated you telling me."

She looked across the parking lot to his truck as if she couldn't wait to leave.

"Next week will be fun, don't you think?" he said. "We'll get to do the crumb coat and everything."

She looked back at him, seeming to finally relax. "Mine will probably look like the rocky side of a mountain when I'm through with it."

"Even ugly cakes taste good in my book."

She'd started toward the truck again, but she glanced back at him. "Don't ever let your mom hear you say that."

"That wouldn't go over too well, would it?"

Logan caught up with her as she reached the truck, but he found that he wasn't ready to go home, or at least to take Caroline back to her mother's house. He wasn't prepared to analyze his hesitancy other than to say that she was his friend. He couldn't go through his whole life without some of those.

He stared up at the sky, stalling. "It's such a nice night. Do you want to take a walk downtown or something?"

Caroline put her hand on the truck door handle instead. "I really should be getting home."

"Looking forward to more time on your mom's sofa?"

It wasn't fair for him to push one of her hot buttons to get her to stay, but he couldn't resist.

Her hand fell to her side as she turned to face him. "Well, when you put it that way."

"Should I be offended by your lack of enthusiasm?"

Caroline shook her head. "I'm just a little tired. But you're right. It's a perfect night for a walk. Besides, if I go home earlier, I'll just be trying sooner to get a turn in the bathroom while Jenna's in there applying another one of her invigorating face masks."

"She does stuff like that?" He gestured for her to lead the way, but instead of following, he fell into step next to her. He tried to ignore the impulse to take her hand as they walked. Was that what he usually wanted to do when he was with his friends? Even really close friends?

"Remember Jenna? She's the queen of shoppers and guinea pig for every new face cream or eye-popping mascara." Caroline passed the first of the downtown shops, glancing in a store window filled with various styles of walking shoes.

"You don't use a lot of that makeup stuff, do you?"

She chuckled but didn't look back at him as they passed a second store. This one had antique and modern, digital cameras in the window. "As little as I can get by with."

"You don't need any at all."

"You're my friend. You have to say that."

The truth was that as her friend he shouldn't have noticed, so he was grateful she hadn't taken him seriously. Or at least if she had, she'd played it off like a pro.

Farther up the street, they approached Markston

Bridal, and she paused to look at the two mannequins, a bride in a froufrou wedding gown and a groom in a black tuxedo.

"Dylan and I are supposed to rent our monkey suits from here," he said. "Are you and Jenna getting your getups here, too?"

"It *is* the only bridal shop in town," she said, wrinkling her nose at the mannequin's gown. "Remember last year when Haley had her gown and our bridesmaids' dresses up for consignment sale here after the broken engagement?"

"But then Matthew made sure Haley and the rest of you made good use of them." He watched her for several long seconds until she started fidgeting.

"What are you looking at?" she asked, still staring at the window.

"I was just wondering how you feel about being in the wedding."

"You asked me that before. Remember, I told you I was worried they were rushing—"

"I mean how do you *really* feel about it with your being antimarriage and all?"

She did look up this time. "Where did you get the idea that I'm antimarriage?"

"Oh, I don't know, maybe all those speeches you gave Haley about not needing a man in her life after that guy broke off their engagement. And your idea to have a 'single-gal shower' since there was no way you were going down any aisle."

"How do you…"

When her words trailed off as she answered her own question, he grinned. "Remember, our moms talk. A lot."

"How could I ever forget. But for the record, I'm not

antimarriage. It just isn't for everyone. For example, someone as career-focused as I am."

"Wow. Some guy must have really done a number on you."

Caroline crossed her arms over her chest. If looks could kill, that one would have at least left a mark. "Why is it that when people see a bachelor, they assume it's by choice, and then any happily single woman must have been wronged by some man?"

Logan watched for a few seconds longer. Her unwillingness to look him in the eye was telling. "I'm not asking about all single women. Just you."

Caroline did meet his gaze now, and the stark look in her eyes unnerved him.

"I was engaged once. In college."

He swallowed. If she'd told him she'd made up the story about her company downsizing and that she'd been fired for incompetence, he wouldn't have been more surprised.

"How is it that I don't already know about this?"

"I didn't tell anyone. Even my sisters."

That she smiled at the memory made him uncomfortable. He had no claim on her, no right to be jealous of any man in her past or present, but he couldn't deny that he was.

"What happened?" He couldn't resist prodding when she didn't say more. When had he ever been curious enough to know more than the basics about any woman?

"I'll tell you that story someday when we both need a good laugh."

He would have told her that he could use a laugh now, but he doubted it would get her to say more. He already knew how stubborn she could be. He should just be satisfied that she'd already shared more with him than she had with anyone, including her sisters.

"Well, Mr. Best Man, I've told you my deep, dark secret, so when are you going to tell me yours?"

"Tell you what?"

"Why you hate weddings."

"I never—"

She started shaking her head before he could finish. "You said it yourself when Dylan asked you to be in the wedding. I believe you said, 'You know how much I *love* weddings.'"

"You see. I never said I hate them." He flashed one of his best smiles, one that would have worked on any woman except Caroline Scott. She just continued watching him, tapping her fingers on the display window.

"Fine. It's not weddings I have a problem with. I just don't have all that much faith in marriage as a long-term institution."

Caroline seemed to consider what he'd said.

"I can see that your experiences might have led you to believe that," she began. "Your dad deserted your family, forcing your mom to raise you and your brothers alone. Then Matthew's first wife did the same thing, leaving him with Lizzie when she was just a baby."

"A couple of good examples, don't you think?" Logan tried not to look uncomfortable as she stated his personal history without so much as flinching. When had he lost the upper hand in this conversation, anyway? He'd done a good job of avoiding talking about his father for years, and he wasn't about to start now.

"Maybe you do have some examples, but are you so cynical that you really believe that Matthew and Haley won't make it even after Haley adopted Lizzie or that Dylan and Jenna don't have a chance?"

"Jury's still out on both couples," he said.

"I think they'll surprise you."

Logan couldn't help but smile over her confidence in their siblings' futures. Who knew that there was a romantic hidden beneath her facade of cynicism? He'd discovered so many unexpected facets to Caroline over these past few weeks. Layers just begging for further study.

That secret engagement of hers was just one of those things. He wanted to know the whole story, whether either of them needed a laugh or not. Mostly he wanted to know why any man who'd been privileged enough to win Caroline's heart would have been so foolish as to let her go.

Somehow though, he doubted that even that answer would be enough to satisfy his need to know everything about her. He watched as Caroline continued on ahead of him toward Markston's only bookstore, A Good Read. When she turned back and caught him watching, a startled expression appeared on her face.

What was he doing? Did he need a reminder of who he was dealing with here? This was Caroline Scott, the only woman he knew who was more opposed to relationships and marriage than he was. Did he need to remember again just how different they were? She had all these big goals that made him think of high-rise buildings and expense accounts when his tastes were simple and his needs were few.

He was on dangerous ground, and he knew it. But it was more than just the possibility that he might be like his father and break someone's heart. He was beginning to worry about his own heart, as well. No matter how much he tried to keep his distance, she drew him in like a moth to a flame. Like the moth, he might learn the hard way that if he came too close to the flame, he might get burned.

Chapter Nine

"You look like a million bucks today." Trina hurried across the hospital room and bent in front of Amy's wheelchair to kiss her cheek.

"After...taxes," Amy answered into her hair.

Trina pulled back and gently gripped her friend's upper arms, studying her face. She almost expected to see Amy's mischievous smile as proof that this difficult time had all been a bad dream, but Amy still looked back at her without expression.

Though her heart squeezed with loss, Trina didn't miss a beat. "Well, aren't you just the comedienne?"

"I try."

Stepping to the wall, Trina pulled a chair over to face the wheelchair where Amy sat for a portion of each morning and afternoon. She sat and took hold of Amy's good hand. She refused to be disappointed. This was an amazing development. Amy had been joking with her. It was a sign that Amy's sense of humor hadn't been a casualty of her stroke as they'd first worried, and Trina couldn't have felt more blessed.

"How many steps did you take today?" Trina repeated

the same question she asked each day on her visits. They always discussed Amy's health first before moving on to a discussion of the bakery.

Amy shook her head. "No. Want to talk…about the wedding."

"Okay," Trina said with a chuckle. "I should have known you would be more interested in how the wedding plans were coming."

"Aren't you?"

"Of course, but I want to know how you're doing, too." Trina patted her friend's hand. "We want to make sure you're in top form so you can be there."

"I'll be there."

"I know you will, and I can't wait."

Trina filled her in on some of the wedding plans—the dress colors, the music and, of course, the cake. Amy leaned forward in her wheelchair, her eyes almost bright with interest. Her recovery had been coming in small steps, but the upcoming wedding had invigorated her spirit and maybe even her healing process.

"Really…going to happen."

"The wedding?" Trina was grinning big enough for the both of them. "It sure took Jenna and Dylan long enough to get around to it, but in a few weeks we'll have another married couple on our hands."

"Matchmakers."

"Amazing matchmakers." Still holding Amy's good hand, Trina reached out with her other hand and touched her friend's weaker arm that lay curled against her robe.

"Caroline?"

"She's still searching for that new job, but she's doing okay. She hasn't even complained about being the maid of honor, and she's been a trooper, dealing with Jenna's fussy planning."

"Logan?"

"I keep telling you he's fine. He's definitely done you proud at the bakery."

But she must not have been answering the question the way Amy hoped she would because Amy shook her head. "No. Logan…and the wedding?"

Trina released her friend's hands. "Oh. That. He's an unlikely best man, but he's been a good sport about it."

"Need to…find matches."

"And we will in time. For Logan and for Caroline. As soon as you're home, we'll get right back to finding matches for our two remaining single children, but for right now I want you to concentrate on getting better." Trina gave her biggest grin. "And getting ready for this wedding."

"Frank Kellam?"

At the name of her fellow church member, Trina blinked. "What? Why are you asking about him? Did he come to visit you?" She shot a glance at the door. "Wait. Did one of our kids say something about him? They were joking about matchmaking, and…"

Trina let her words trail away as she noticed the confusion in Amy's eyes.

"Oh. Were you asking if he and the other church members were invited to the wedding?" When her friend nodded, Trina cleared her throat. "Yes. Dylan and Jenna invited the whole congregation."

Trina braced herself for more uncomfortable questions, but Amy dropped the subject. She even let Trina comb her hair and use water to make it lie in place. Trina tried to tell herself she was relieved because she could finally focus on more important matters such as Amy's recovery, but it was more than that and she knew it.

Whether just by accident or with encouragement from their children, Amy had brought up the name of a man who wanted to see her socially. How could any of them think she might be ready to date him or any man?

Well, she wasn't ready and doubted she ever would be. Only a little more than two years had passed since Gary's death. She was no romantic, but even she understood that lifetime love only happened once in a lifetime. Memories were a poor substitute for his sturdy arms around her, but she'd learned to live with them, and she wished the others would just leave her alone.

As Trina rubbed lotion on her friend's hands, she felt as if her heart was breaking. This was the kind of problem she would have shared with her best friend. Amy would have understood why Trina couldn't even fathom the idea of spending time with another man, how it would feel like she was betraying Gary and the life they'd built together.

But she couldn't talk to Amy about this, not when Amy's challenges were so much more significant, her hurdles towering over Trina's mere bumps in the road of life. That she couldn't share thoughts like these only made her hurt feel more profound. Her friend with whom she'd shared a lifetime of memories was in some ways absent from her life.

Her reasons were selfish, perhaps, but she was even more determined to find that friend again, more important, to help Amy find herself. Trina could worry about her own social life later.

* * *

Caroline had just finished inputting the week's receipts into the software program when a commotion of loud voices and clanging pans started in the kitchen. She leaped out of her rolling chair so quickly that she made a bang of her own when it rolled backward and crashed into the filing cabinet. Not bothering to stop and right the chair, she rushed out the door and down the short hall to the kitchen.

"What's going on in here?"

The kitchen looked like a disaster with used cake pans and utensils filling the sink and counters still decorated with colorful splatters of frosting. Caroline didn't have to cross the floor to guess that her shoes would stick to it when she did.

"We're celebrating," Logan announced and then did a drumbeat on a cake pan with a rubber spatula. "We just delivered the last wedding cake for June, and we got it there in one piece despite a pothole the size of Texas on the corner of Washington and Drake."

Kamie crossed the room, pounding one of the beaters from the industrial-sized mixer against the inside of a steel bowl. She didn't seem to mind that they'd had to stay almost to dinnertime to finish the last cake for an evening wedding.

"We survived wedding month," Kamie said.

"Yeah, we made it," Margie cheered. "We even have new orders for nearly every weekend through Christmas."

"Did any of you ever doubt it?" Caroline asked and then held up her hand. "No. Don't answer that. Anyway, I'm sure Mrs. Warren will be proud of everyone's hard work."

"She'll be especially proud of you two," Kamie said when she stopped pounding.

"Well, thank you, Kamie." Logan smiled at both of the decorators.

As he moved to the sink to start rinsing the pans and placing them in the dish sanitizer, Logan exchanged a look with Caroline and grinned. She couldn't help smiling back at him. If there was one thing she could say about Logan, it was that he had an ability to win over his critics, including her.

"You ladies have done a great job today. If you want to get out of here, I'll clean up the mess and lock up for the night," he said.

"That sounds like a great idea to me," Margie said. She linked her arm though Kamie's, and the two of them hurried out the back door.

Caroline stared after them before turning back to Logan. "Well, you didn't have to tell them twice."

"Aren't you going with them? This is going to take a while."

"I figured you could use the help." At his skeptical glance, she added, "And my calendar is pretty clear."

It was about as good as any excuse she'd used so many evenings lately to hang out with him at the bakery. They'd worked together every night they weren't visiting his mother in the long-term rehabilitation center or attending the cake-decorating class. She appreciated that every night he pretended to be surprised to see her.

This time he pressed his lips together to keep from smiling. "I'm sure Jenna can find you some chore to do for the wedding. Maybe you can help her pick table decorations and party favors or something."

"Oh, no thank you. I'll just suffer through doing the cleaning here."

Caroline expected Logan to kid her about her lack of plans on a Saturday night, but he only returned to rinsing the pans. To make herself useful, she started collecting some of the empty decorator bags and tips.

"It looks like there was a tornado in here."

"It was crazy when we were trying to get those three cakes out."

"We?" She raised a brow. They'd only had a few sessions of their cake-decorating class so far. He'd already proven he was skilled at piping, and his crumb coats weren't half-bad, but had he already been brave enough to try out his skills on a real wedding cake?

Logan shook his head. "I just supervised. I haven't let the ladies in on our little secret yet."

Caroline wasn't sure why, but it pleased her that he'd referred to the cake-decorating class as *their* secret instead of only his. For reasons she didn't want to analyze, she liked the idea that the project belonged to the two of them. "But you do seem to have finally won over all the employees."

"You think so? I knew my charms would eventually get through to them. They always work on women."

He flashed Caroline a dimpled smile that would have done the trick if all of Logan's hard work hadn't already convinced the critics to come over to his side.

She rolled her eyes. "Whatever you say, Logan."

"Well, not every woman…but most."

Though she shook her head over his silliness, she couldn't help but smile. He was probably right. Most. Even those who'd promised themselves they would remain immune to his charms. Definitely most.

"Wait a minute," she said as realization dawned. "It's Saturday night. This is the second time I've seen you here on a Saturday night when you could have been out on a date."

"What's wrong with that? You're here."

"I'm not 'Logan-the-lady-killer.'"

She cringed after she said it but felt even more uncomfortable when he didn't say anything. With dread she turned back to him, and, as she'd predicted, he was grinning at her.

"'Logan-the-lady-killer,' huh?"

"That's what your brothers call you."

"They do?"

He tilted his head back and forth as if trying on the name for the first time. A disturbing feeling settled inside her gut as she remembered "Ranger Logan," one of Logan's other nicknames that hadn't been quite accurate.

"I suppose it fits as long as you don't take it literally." The side of Logan's mouth lifted. "Those women were very much alive when I took them home. If anything happened to them after I left, well, I..."

"Very funny. You know what I meant."

"Okay, I've dated a lot of women. But in my defense I can say that I haven't treated them as ruthlessly as that name suggests." He must have read her confusion because he explained, "I'm not much for second dates."

Strange how his clarification confused her even more. She'd always thought of him as someone like Kevin, who broke hearts for sport, but it didn't sound as if he ever became invested enough to hurt anyone.

"But you always had dates whenever we tried to make

Warren-Scott family plans," she began, trying to sound casual. "And then lately…"

"I know. I haven't lived up to my rep. I've had more important stuff on my mind these last few weeks."

"You have been pretty focused on being there for your mom and running her business."

She waited for him to say more, but he only nodded and then started toward the storage room. Pulling out the bottle of disinfectant, she sprayed the counter and started wiping. From behind her, she could hear Logan returning, pulling the squeaky-wheeled bucket and mop along with him.

"It's more than that."

"What?" Caroline turned to find him using the wringer to squeeze water from the mop.

"The reason I've been taking a break from the dating scene."

"But you did go on a date that one Sunday afternoon—" Though Caroline stopped herself, it wasn't soon enough to keep Logan from looking at her strangely.

"You remember that? It was more a date with a place than a person. I'll have to take you there someday."

Instead of saying more, Logan wrung out the mop again and started washing the floor near the ovens.

"Now wait a minute," she said. "I get the feeling you were just about to tell me something momentous."

"Oh," Logan said, shaking his head. "Forget it."

Caroline planted her hands on her hips. "Are you kidding? This might be the most fascinating tidbit I've ever learned about the infamous Logan Warren, and if you think I'm going to let it go now, then you obviously don't know how determined I can be."

"Believe me, I know." He dropped the mop back

in the bucket and blew out a heavy breath. "I'm just tired."

"Why didn't you say so? Go home. I can do all this."

But he started shaking his head. "No, I mean that's why I'm stepping back from dating. I'm tired of a lot of things. Of too many first dates. Of trying to impress women instead of really getting to know them. Even of not having anyone I can call when I get home at night."

Caroline just stared at him, somehow managing to keep her mouth from falling open. She didn't have to guess to know that he'd never said these things to anyone else, and she couldn't have been more surprised that he'd chosen to share them with her.

Logan wore the stark look of a man who'd spent little time alone but just might be as lonely as she was. And she could finally admit that she *was* lonely.

Her heart reached out to him with an intensity that shocked her. She was glad for the wet rubber gloves she wore because those and sheer determination were the only things that kept her from rushing over to him and wrapping her arms around him. He wouldn't appreciate the impulse or the soggy, pitying hug.

But was it only compassion she felt for him? she asked herself as she dragged her gaze away from him. It couldn't be more. This was Logan Warren, and there were so many reasons why keeping her distance from him would be in her best interest. But those reasons suddenly felt like a water balloon riddled with holes. The lines between friendship and something more had blurred for her, and she needed to draw clear lines again and fast.

When she glanced at him again, he wore a sheepish grin.

"That was too heavy for cleaning conversation."

"Too heavy? No. Surprising? Yes."

"My mother's stroke opened my eyes about a lot of things. Like wasting time. Life is too short for that."

"You're right about that." Her father's image slipped into her thoughts, and as if her mind turned a page, she saw Mrs. Warren's face, as well.

"Thinking about your dad again?"

She nodded, no longer surprised that Logan read her so easily. He might be the most unlikely person to be in tune with her, but he was, and it was as simple as that. "About a lot of things."

Strangely, she felt as if she was beginning to know him, too, not the surface things she'd always heard about him, but the real Logan, who was a caring, articulate man. A person she wanted to know better.

"I've always heard people say that when you're on your deathbed, you'll never wish you'd spent more time at the office," he said.

"That's a tough thing for someone like me to hear." Having finished wiping down the counters, she started cleaning off the industrial mixer. "I planned to break through the corporate glass ceiling by thirty."

"How's that working out for you?"

She frowned as she looked back at him from the mixer, but she softened when he started chuckling. "Well, there's been a bump in the road, but I'll get there. Might have to wait until…oh…thirty-two." She hoped he didn't ask her about the job search that had stalled lately. She had no idea what she would say if he asked her why.

"That old?"

But he turned away from her after he said it and then was suddenly focused on finishing the mopping, as if their conversation had bothered him somehow. She guessed that he was still uncomfortable about having opened up to her.

To give him space, she moved from the kitchen to the dining area, where she began emptying the bakery case of the leftover cookies, cupcakes and cakes. Those things would need to be delivered to Shared Blessings soup kitchen after they finished up here. She'd only finished the first case before he came through the swinging door with his bucket, joining her in the space out front where they'd spent several evenings lately.

"Are you following me?" she asked.

"Why would I do that?"

As she bent to retrieve a lonely carrot cake from the front of the case, she gave him a silly look through the glass. "I don't know," she said as she stood up again. "Maybe because you think that now that you've shared your deep, dark secret that I'll tell you the rest of my story."

"You think I told you my story just to get yours out of you?" He tilted his head as if considering. "Well, it is a good idea, but I'm not good at that whole manipulation thing. Maybe they teach that in business school."

He grinned over his pithy line, but then he turned serious. "You'll tell me when you're ready."

Caroline swallowed. He'd just said he wasn't going to push her, and suddenly she was tempted to tell him far more than just about her disastrous engagement. Like that she was beginning to have feelings for him, feelings that were more startling and frightening than anything she remembered experiencing with her ex-fiancé.

"Well, we'd better finish up here and get the stuff over to Shared Blessings because I do have a date tonight."

"You do?" She hated the shock in her voice and her sudden clumsiness that made her nearly drop the box she'd just stuffed with leftover cupcakes.

"With Mom," he explained quickly. "I'm giving Matthew and Dylan the night off, so Mom and I will hang out and watch a little TV."

Caroline didn't want to acknowledge the sigh of relief that she released in tiny bursts.

"I can't wait to celebrate with her that we survived June. But now we have July and August and— Maybe I won't tell her that."

"Probably shouldn't."

She shouldn't have been thinking any of the things she had, either. At least one of them had his priorities straight—still remembered they were here to help his mother—and it clearly wasn't her. She needed to follow his example and find her own focus again. She should spend the rest of her Saturday night putting out more resumes. They weren't exciting plans, but her rental and utility bills for her apartment weren't going anywhere, and her banking account was dwindling fast.

"You can come along if you want," he said.

"I really shouldn't, but—"

"Have more exciting plans?"

"Not exactly." Suddenly, the thought of spending the evening sitting in front of her mother's desktop computer held even less appeal.

"Then come. You know how much Mom enjoys your visits."

Her lips were already shaped for her to say "no" when Logan tilted his head to the side. "Please. For me."

She knew she'd lost the fight the moment he grinned and his dimples popped. She was just trying to be there for her friend, just as Logan was being there for his mother, she told herself, but the thought didn't ring true. The truth was enough to send her racing back up Interstate 65 to Chicago. She would make any excuse today to spend more time with Logan Warren.

Chapter Ten

Caroline stared at herself in the full-length mirror and had the sudden urge to do a girlish spin to see the midnight-blue, A-line gown float out around her ankles. Only the pins the seamstress had been inserting at the hemline kept her from trying out the spin.

"Oh, Caroline. You look amazing."

That Haley stared at her with that same awed little-sister look she used to have when they were children made Caroline smile at her reflection. Caroline traced her fingertips over smooth silk, following the tiny dip in the strapless gown's sweetheart neckline.

She'd never thought of herself as the fairy-tale type. She'd always related easier to the Elizabeth Bennetts from fiction rather than Cinderella or the Little Mermaid. But the woman staring back at her from that mirror looked like a princess, even to her. And her fingers tingled at the thought of the handsome, tuxedo-clad prince who would be escorting her down the aisle.

"It isn't bad, is it?" Jenna said as she swished into the room, the delicate train of her simple silk bridal gown bunched up over her arm.

"Oh, Jenna. You look beautiful." Haley shifted in the armchair they'd brought into the dressing room so she could sit more comfortably. She studied Jenna from the round neckline to the appliques at the bottom of her full skirt and then wiped her eyes with the back of her hand.

"Haley, dear. Are you crying again?" Trina, who'd trailed in behind Jenna, took a few tissues from a box on a nearby table and handed them to her youngest daughter. "Amy's usually the one who cries over weddings."

"Don't worry, Mom. Mrs. Warren will be there, crying away this time, too," Jenna told her as she stepped up behind Caroline, who still stood on the seamstress's pedestal. "Haley here will probably join her. She's weepy because of the baby."

Caroline was feeling a little misty-eyed herself, and she had no excuse other than that she'd recently developed a soft spot for weddings. Not about to admit that to anyone, she cleared her throat. "Here. Let me get out of your way."

Jenna shook her head. "Not until we've properly admired you."

"But you're the bride," Caroline said, already backing off the step.

"That's right. I am, and I get to have my way."

Caroline rolled her eyes, but she dutifully stepped back on the pedestal. She even started spinning slowly when Jenna requested it.

"What are we going to do about Mrs. Warren's and Lizzie's dresses?" Caroline asked as she continued to spin.

Haley finished wiping her eyes and looked back to the mirror. "Lizzie's dress didn't need to be fitted, and we picked a loose-fitting chiffon for Amy so she won't need a fitting, either."

Jenna was still watching Caroline in the mirror. "Don't you guys think I did a great job of matching the dress to her eye color? And look at how that blue brings out the auburn highlights in her hair."

Rather than answer, the others applauded. Haley even executed a two-finger whistle.

Caroline's cheeks heated. "It sounds like you put more effort into choosing my dress than you did yours."

"Are you kidding?" Jenna said. "I've had my wedding dress picked out since about sixth grade, but yours I had to choose on short notice."

"Sure, I remember," Caroline told her. "You hung a picture of it on your wall with your teen heartthrob posters."

"I remember, too," Haley chimed. "Jenna and I used to play brides with our fashion dolls, but even then you weren't into all the hoopla about weddings."

"That's not true." Caroline shook her head and then grinned. "But either way, I'm going to like *this* wedding."

"You'd better like this one." Jenna paused to shake a warning finger at her sister. "Remember, I picked out that dress knowing full well you're going to outshine everybody there…including the bride."

"Now that is *not* going to happen, Jenna. Just look at you." Caroline gestured to her sister's gown.

She stepped off the pedestal again so that Jenna could take her place and they could get a good look at her amazing dress. They kept on oohing and aahing over it, even after the seamstress returned and started inserting pins for minor alterations on the dress that was already close to perfect.

"You are a vision, sweetheart," Trina said.

Caroline had to agree, but something her sister had said still bothered her. "Not that it would ever be possible, but why would you want me to outshine you on your wedding day? It's *your* day."

In the mirror, Jenna gave her a knowing smile. "This dress is great, but Dylan would still think I looked beautiful even if I designed my own gown out of paper towels and cotton balls. But we wanted to make sure you look fabulous just in case one of those great guys at the wedding—"

"You can't be serious!"

Caroline didn't realize she'd raised her voice until Jenna's eyes widened. Their mother and Haley stared at her as well, and even the seamstress looked up from where she was kneeling with color-topped straight pins in her mouth. Caroline didn't care. They had no right to remind her about the single men who would be at her sister's wedding when she was having a hard enough time keeping her mind off one of those men in particular.

She cleared her throat and started again. "More matchmaking? I know you think you're being helpful, but this isn't helping."

Catching sight of Haley moving nervously in her chair, Caroline replayed Jenna's words in her thoughts. "Wait. You said *we*. Were you all in on this? Remember, Mom, I told you if you tried again I would put myself up for adoption."

Trina held her hands up in the pose of the innocent. "Don't look at me this time. I had nothing to do with it."

But Caroline did look at her little sister, who was fighting back a grin.

"Haley, you know better than this." She turned to include the bride-to-be in the lecture. "You both know better. You hated it when Mom was trying to match you up with the Warren brothers."

"Match *us* up?" her sisters chorused and then laughed.

"Don't you mean matching *you* up?" Haley glanced at Jenna and their mother conspiratorially. "Isn't it funny how she rewrites history?"

"There wasn't anything funny about it," Caroline said.

Her jaw tightened as they all laughed about some of the most humiliating moments of her life. Jenna was the first to notice that Caroline wasn't laughing.

"Aw, come on." Jenna tilted her head to the side in an endearing pose. "You can laugh about it now, can't you?"

She tilted her head, considering. "Um, no. It's not funny yet."

Jenna started nodding. "Okay, I get that, but you have to understand. Haley and I are just so happy with Matthew and Dylan that we can't help wanting you to be happy, too."

Haley leaned on the arm of the chair and slowly came to her feet. "And if you think about it, if Mom and Mrs. Warren hadn't been trying to match you up with the guys, then maybe we wouldn't have figured out that God wanted us to be with them." She indicated Jenna with a tilt of her head. "For sure, *she* wouldn't have figured it out."

"I'm a slow learner," Jenna said with a shrug.

"You're welcome, I guess, but don't let any misplaced sense of gratitude cloud your judgment here," Caroline said. "I'm already happy. Or at least I will be when I'm back to work, and everything gets back to normal."

Haley studied her closely. "Are you sure about that?"

She bristled because she'd been asking herself the same thing lately. Was she really happy? Was her single life enough for her anymore? Would her life ever return to normal now that she and Logan had crossed paths? Even if she found the perfect job, would she forever be asking herself what if?

"Yes, I'm sure," she answered. "So let it go, will you? Even Mom and Mrs. Warren let it go. Why can't you?"

Jenna only shrugged and then rubbed her side where the pins in the dress's waistline pricked her skin.

Haley grinned. "I wouldn't be so sure Mom and Mrs. Warren have given up entirely, either. Mom might be just biding her time until my mother-in-law is feeling up to their schemes again."

"Who, me?" But Trina chuckled when she said it.

"Come on, guys. This is my life. It isn't a game."

With that Caroline stomped into the farthest dressing room and yanked the curtain shut. The zipper on her dress wouldn't give at first, and it was all she could do not to yank it and possibly tear the delicate fabric. She had to get out of this dress and away from these people, who cared so much and were interfering *too* much in an area they couldn't possibly understand.

As soon as she had pulled on her khakis and her white blouse and had hung her dress back in its garment bag, she pulled open the curtain again. Her sisters and mother were standing outside the dressing area, Jenna still in her bridal gown, waiting for her.

"I have to get back to the bakery. We're having a big supplies delivery this afternoon, and I told Logan I would try to get back."

"Wait, Caroline." Haley launched herself into her sister's arms. "We're sorry. It's just—"

"I know. I know. It's okay."

"We won't bring it up again. Promise." Jenna swished forward and wrapped her older sister in her arms. "But we won't be able to help it if you get noticed in that dress. That's all on you."

"I'll take my chances, then." Caroline shook her head.

Though the mood had lightened, Caroline still couldn't get out of the bridal shop soon enough. She hated that her sisters' meager attempt at matchmaking bothered her so much. It shouldn't even have surprised her that they would take up their mother's matchmaking hobby, especially now that they'd both found such happiness.

But it did bother her, more than she cared to admit. Not because they were just like their mother in ignoring her choice to remain a single woman. Not even because they had all but planned to show off her straight teeth to market her as a potential bride to wedding guests. Her reason was so much simpler than that and more complex and confusing at the same time. They hadn't once considered matching her with the best man.

"Do we get to use the sparklers yet, Uncle Logan?"

"What?" Logan glance down at Lizzie, who had folded her hands in a pleading pose and was looking up at him with a hopeful gaze. "Oh. Sorry, sweetie. We won't see those until after we leave the center. It's not dark yet."

"But why?"

Her frown made him chuckle. His goals and those of his niece were at odds today. She was in a hurry for darkness to come so they could go watch the Markston community fireworks display. He didn't want this day to end.

Even if they were cooking out in the back parking lot of the rehabilitation center instead of the park and even if it was overcast instead of sunny the way the Fourth of July should have been, it was a perfect holiday in his opinion. The whole Warren-Scott clan was finally together again, which gave them a miracle to celebrate along with freedom and independence.

"Lizzie, why don't you come over here and find places to put these little flags," Trina called from the picnic table.

Fireworks forgotten for now, the child skipped over to the table and nabbed a pair of them, becoming a single-child parade as she marched around the lawn chairs.

Near the picnic table, covered in a festive tablecloth, his mother held court in her wheelchair. Maybe the outdoor air had something to do with it, but she looked better than ever, her skin back to its healthy tone, her eyes shiny and bright. She had her new bathrobe secured at her waist and an afghan Haley had made tucked over her lap.

"Wave…Lizzie," Amy said as her granddaughter marched past. She even waved the flag the child handed to her.

Logan's heart squeezed as he watched her. This really

was going to happen. She was going to be okay. Except for the arm that his mother held against her body as if to shield it, she already looked like her old self.

His mother caught him watching her and waved. As he waved back, he heard Dylan calling his name.

"Taking another break?" Dylan turned to flip a few hamburgers on the grill that they'd brought over in Logan's truck.

"I just didn't want to wrestle you for the control of the grill." Logan stepped closer and glanced down at the cooking meat. "Doesn't Mom look great?"

Dylan took a moment to watch her waving her flag, and then he nodded. "She's doing so well. I think she'll be fine for the wedding."

"Are you getting nervous for next Saturday?"

"Nope." The groom-to-be held out his hand. It wasn't trembling at all.

"Not even the part about having to stand up there before God and everyone?" Logan lifted a brow.

"Okay. A little. But only about that. I'm not the performer in the family like you."

"One's enough." Logan took another look at their mother, who was reaching up to pat Haley's rounded belly. "We'd better hurry and get this dinner over with. We can't overtire Mom today if want her to be in top shape for the wedding."

Dylan waved away his worries. "She'll be fine. The wedding will be fine. It'll all be great."

Logan had to smile at his love-struck brother. "Well, this cookout is going to be about as great as the last one if you burn everything again."

"Hey, don't blame me for that." Dylan lifted both

hands, one of them still holding a spatula. "Nobody was watching the grill that day."

"Whatever you say."

"Guys, do you need me to take over here?"

Logan hadn't needed to hear her voice to know that it was Caroline who'd approached from behind him. He would sense her presence even if he was blindfolded and he wore earplugs and nose plugs. She'd become a sixth sense for him, her nearness like a touch on his skin and a warmth in his chest, and even if it scared him to death, he didn't want it to stop.

Caroline looked so fresh today, her skin free of makeup and her hair pulled back from her face and secured with a clip at her nape. From her blue holiday T-shirt to her khaki shorts and her little socks and tennis shoes, she looked like a teenager.

Logan tried to come up with something clever to say, and, for once, he had nothing. Instead, he cleared his throat and looked to Dylan to fill the silence.

Dylan looked at him with surprise before he turned back to Caroline. "Are you kidding? This is male territory you're entering here. Don't emasculate us by trying to take away our grilling tools."

Caroline snapped her fingers. "I should have known. Here I'd been thinking that the old boys' club did all their important business transactions in the corporate men's room or on the links, but all along the good stuff was happening around the grill."

"I don't know about corporate America, but around here we're just competing to see who can make a superior steak," Logan said. He leaned over conspiratorially to her. "Just in case you don't already know the answer to that, it's me."

Caroline sank her front teeth into her bottom lip and looked past him to Dylan before she answered again. "It's just like when you two were kids. Always competing. Are you planning a spitball contest next?"

"We might, so watch out."

Her mother called her over then, so Caroline continued to the picnic table, leaving Logan alone with his obviously curious brother. Logan considered finding an excuse to get away, too, but he wasn't fast enough.

"What was that all about?"

"I don't know what you're talking about." Logan didn't look at him, focusing on the women bustling around the picnic table.

"Only that there were enough sparks flying around here to start a fire nowhere near the grill."

"You're imagining things, brother."

"Maybe," Dylan said in a tone that suggested he was pretty sure he wasn't imagining anything. "I hope you know what you're doing."

Logan only made an affirmative sound since any real response would open him to more questions he wasn't prepared to answer.

Dylan must have figured he wasn't likely to hear more because he continued, "Well, whatever you're planning, be careful. No matter how much we wish it otherwise, people don't usually change who they are."

"Jenna did."

Dylan nodded at his brother's mention of Jenna's transformation last summer, but then he shrugged as if that didn't affect what he'd said before. "Hey, can you do this? I have to go help Jenna with the ketchup and mustard."

Logan accepted the spatula into his hand. Whether

his brother had been talking about him or Caroline in his comment about change, he wasn't sure, but the words struck home either way. He was who he was, and she was who she was, and neither of them was likely to change.

Whatever you're planning... Again, his brother's words struck him. Was he really planning anything? Or would he choose to let the tide take him to her no matter how unwise the decision, no matter how much of a mistake it would probably be?

Managing to finish the meat without burning it, Logan carried the tray of hotdogs and hamburgers over to the table, where the others gathered with Amy's wheelchair parked at the end. Logan slipped onto one of the benches, and Caroline sat next to him in the only remaining empty spot at the table.

Trina took hold of her best friend's frail left hand, and then she reached out for Matthew's hand on the other side. Soon, the whole group was connected in a circle that began and ended with Amy Warren. Maybe a little different, but it was a Warren-Scott dinner.

This was what Logan had hoped and prayed for. So why during this important moment was he spending all his energy trying to ignore how soft, how small and delicate Caroline's hand felt in his? Trying not to think about how right it felt with this one woman at his side?

As if she knew he wasn't paying attention, Trina cleared her throat and began the blessing.

"Father God, thank You for looking down on us today," Trina prayed. "Thank You for Your healing power that You've showered on our dear Amy. Please continue to work Your miracles with her and in all of our hearts."

Trina stopped as she and his mother often did when they wanted to offer the others an opportunity to contribute to the prayer. Usually Matthew would have picked up next, but something felt different to Logan today. He felt compelled to speak next.

"Lord, thank You for bringing us all together again. Thank You for the gift of each Scott and each Warren sitting around this table—even those we have yet to meet. Thank You for relationships that last a lifetime."

He stopped there before he said too much, though he suspected he might have already. For several seconds, no one said anything, as if they were either digesting his words or waiting for the next one to speak.

"Thank you, Jesus, for the food," Lizzie said in a small voice. "Amen."

As soon as they opened their eyes, they all started laughing. Lizzie laughed the loudest.

With regret, Logan released Caroline's hand, but when he gave her a sidelong glance, he caught her watching him. If shock, need and uncertainty could all be reflected in a single gaze, those were the things he thought he saw in her eyes. It was all he could do not to reach out to her again in front of all their relatives and beg her to tell him what she was thinking. He'd thought his feelings for her had been one-sided. Was he wrong?

"Were you in a hurry to finish that prayer?" Jenna asked her niece as she pulled one of her pigtails.

"I'm hungry." Lizzie grinned and reached for a hamburger bun.

"Me, too," Matthew leaned over and snuggled against

his daughter's ear, making her giggle again. "I didn't think Uncle Logan was ever going to be finished."

"Me, neither." Lizzie giggled.

Dylan passed the tray of meat down to some of the others. "That was a new thing. Usually Matthew's the one who always prays until all the food gets cold."

"Sorry about that." Logan held his hands wide. "I got a little long-winded."

The others laughed and then got down to the business of passing dishes of deviled eggs, potato salad and chips around the table and devouring those things, plus the hotdogs and hamburgers.

As Logan filled his plate, he could sense Dylan watching him, but he refused to look at him. He was having enough trouble trying to keep from staring at the amazing woman seated next to him and to keep from coming out of his seat when her elbow accidentally touched his to worry about his brother's questions. They would all be answered soon enough. One way or another.

He'd lost his appetite, but he forced himself to take a few bites anyway. The sooner they finished the meal and cleaned up, the sooner they could get to Markston Central High School's football field for the fireworks. He no longer resented time passing because he was looking forward to the chance to talk to Caroline. This time he would do all the talking.

Finally, Logan relaxed into his seat and started eating with gusto. He even participated in the enthusiastic dinner conversation that was part of Warren-Scott tradition. It was freeing to have a plan. For the first time in weeks, he knew exactly what he was going to do.

Chapter Eleven

The evening sky exploded with light and color, but Caroline was too unsettled to marvel at the pyrotechnics as she rested on one of her mother's quilts among a sea of holiday revelers. Though applause broke out around her, she hardly noticed the starbursts, geometric shapes and the sparkling flag that lit the sky.

She was too busy trying not to notice—and noticing nonetheless—every movement of a particular fireworks fan farther down on their group's line of blankets.

"Wow, did you see that one?" Jenna elbowed her in case she hadn't.

"Uh, yeah. That was great," she answered, but she would have been hard-pressed to describe the colors if quizzed on it. "Too bad Mom was too tired to join us. She's going to be sorry she missed this."

Caroline shifted to make her lap a more comfortable pillow for Lizzie, who'd been so excited to see the fireworks but had settled in for a snooze after only the first few explosions.

Jenna reached down to brush their niece's head. "How can she sleep through this?"

"That's the worry-free sleep of the young."

"Must be nice to sleep like a stone the way she does." Jenna adjusted the sweatshirt they'd draped over Lizzie's little body before she looked up. "Hey, what do you have to lose sleep over? You're not planning a wedding."

Caroline sat up, startling Lizzie, but the child only snuggled closer and continued dozing. "I don't know. Unemployment, maybe." That wasn't even close to the whole story, but she hoped her sister would accept it.

"Oh. Right," Jenna said with a nervous giggle. "Forgot about that. Have you heard back from any of the companies you've approached?"

"Not many. I've received a few rejection letters, but I'm still waiting to hear from most of them." She shifted her position, trying to get comfortable without waking the child. "I can't live with Mom forever, you know."

"Why not? Her spare bedroom will even be free after—" Jenna stopped herself as if a thought had struck. "Oh, my. Can you believe Dylan and I are going to be husband and wife in only eight days?"

"It's about time."

Caroline smiled up into the vast blanket of twinkling lights. With the clock ticking down to the wedding, it had been easy to distract Jenna from her question. If only she could find a way to divert her own attention from the man who'd been at the center of her thoughts for days.

Automatically, her gaze returned to Logan, who sat next to Matthew and Haley. He was looking back at her, just as he had been every time she'd sneaked a peek all night. Did he ever stop watching her, or could he just sense when she was about to look at him so he could catch her in the act? Either way, she was all flustered like a teenager with a secret crush. If this was a crush, she was doing a lousy job of keeping it a secret.

She looked up in time to see the sky awash with light in the grand finale. Booms continued to pound in her ears as the last remnants of color and light drifted toward the ground. At once, the stadium lights of the football field started to come to life, first in a dull glow and then brighter to guide spectators to the parking lot.

Matthew reached Caroline first and crouched next to her, reaching for his daughter. "Here, let me get her."

Caroline stood on unsteady legs as one of her limbs had gone to sleep beneath the weight of the sleeping child. Immediately, there was a hand beneath her elbow.

"Need a little help there?" Logan asked.

"No, I'm fine." But she didn't shake his hand away as she would have a month before. She wasn't even offended by his assistance.

Dylan stepped closer, a folded blanket under his arm. "Who's going in which car?"

Caroline noticed first that Logan's hand fell away from her arm and then that the two brothers exchanged an odd look that she guessed had everything to do with her.

"I don't care who I go with, but Mom took my car, and it's an awfully long walk back to her house, so..." Caroline let her words trail off, hoping that someone would volunteer.

"I guess we could take you since we're going to the same house," Dylan said, frowning.

Matthew snickered. "And miss out on a chance for that private good-night kiss with Jenna? That would be a cruel thing for us to do to the almost newlyweds." He tilted his head so it brushed against Haley's as she snuggled against his side. "Remember how we used to be?"

"What do you mean *used to be?*" Dylan said.

Haley shook her head. "Anyway, we can take you."

"Why would you do that?" Logan wanted to know. "It's out of your way to go by there. And you have to get Lizzie home to bed. I'll take Caroline."

"You're sure?" Jenna asked, not seeming upset with the idea of having a few minutes of alone time with Dylan.

"It's on my way," Logan said without inflection, but he looked away when Dylan glanced at him.

Caroline didn't say anything—wasn't sure she could. She'd sensed that something was different with Logan tonight, and the anticipation inside her seemed to confirm it. He was only giving her a lift home. She'd done the same thing for him a few times when he'd ridden his motorcycle to work on sunshiny mornings that produced rainy afternoons.

But this was different. She understood that deep in her gut. She almost expected Logan to explain why as they trudged in silence to his truck, but he was silent. Once he'd opened the door for her and climbed in on the driver's side, she couldn't take the silence anymore.

"Why do I get the feeling I've just been passed around like an unwanted storage box?"

"Why do you think that?" He turned on his lights and inched the truck forward, but it would be a while before he could move into the line of cars heading toward the parking lot exit. "I can still wave down Dylan and Jenna if you're determined to be a third wheel."

"No, thanks." She chuckled. "I do wonder why you volunteered to take me instead of letting Matthew and Haley do it. It's not really that much farther for them."

Logan wasn't looking at her as he finally got a break in traffic. He waved at the other driver and pulled into the line. "They have Lizzie. And Haley had to be tired."

"That was nice of you."

"I didn't do it to be nice."

"Then why did you?" Caroline studied his profile, but his expression didn't give anything away. The anticipation she'd felt earlier might turn to foreboding if he didn't speak up soon.

"I thought you and I should talk."

"Okay. Let's talk."

But instead of doing that, he became as quiet as he'd been on the walk to his truck. He drove from one end of downtown to the other without so much as clearing his throat. Soon they were on the street in front of her mother's house, and she still didn't know what was so important that he'd felt the need to orchestrate the chance to drive her home.

"Logan? Didn't you want to talk?"

"In a minute."

He passed Dylan's car, which was parked right in front of the house, and stopped his truck a few houses farther up the street. After he shut off the engine, he turned in his seat to face her.

"I didn't think it would be this hard. I never had trouble with this stuff before."

She opened her mouth to ask him what he was having trouble with, but he lifted a hand to tell her to wait.

"Have I ever mentioned that patience isn't one of your virtues?"

It would take the patience of Job to wait around for him to get to the point, she thought, but remained silent.

"I was talking about how hard a time I'm having asking you out."

Caroline started coughing into her hand, and it took her several seconds before she could control it. Her pulse raced, and her palms were so damp that she had to wipe them on her jeans. "Asking...me...out?"

Logan breathed out a heavy sigh. "You're choking. I guess I should be grateful you didn't start laughing. I guess that's something. But clearly I've lost my touch."

"That's not what I meant. I mean...is that what you're asking? Because maybe we should really think about it before... You know." She pressed her back against the door, fighting the impulse to reach for the door handle and bolt. Only now could she admit to herself that she'd wanted him to ask, and now that he'd done it, all of her uncertainties were lining up against the idea of accepting.

"Come on, Logan. We've known each other all our lives. I can still remember the time—"

"Don't."

He hadn't even raised his voice, and yet the word reverberated off the walls of the truck cab. Caroline stared at him, her hands gripping together in her lap.

"What?" she asked.

"I know this makes you uncomfortable, but I don't want you to come up with some funny story about something I did as a kid or something you did in your babysitter role." He folded his arms. "You're older than I am. We both know that. Now get over it. We stopped being those kids a long time ago."

Caroline blinked. How could she answer him when everything he'd just said about her was true? She opened her mouth, hoping her mind would catch up and give her the words, but finally she gave up and closed it.

"Good," Logan said. "Now I have to know if you would be willing to go out with me on a real date. As us. As the people we are now."

Her pulse pounded in her ears. She was facing a moment of truth, and she realized she'd known the truth all along. "Where do you want to go?"

Logan must have expected an argument to his suggestion because he began, "I don't care if there are good reasons why we shouldn't—"

"That's not what I asked." Caroline surprised herself by sounding confident instead of hesitant, the way she really felt.

"Oh. Right." But then he leaned closer to her, his gaze narrowing. "Is that a yes, then?"

"Yes," she answered in a small voice.

"So…does it make a difference where we go?"

She smiled this time. "No."

Logan smiled back at her. "Then bring your riding boots because tomorrow we're taking a ride out to my favorite place in the world."

It sounded great and scary at the same time. Rather than let him come around the truck to open her door, Caroline let herself out just in time to see Jenna kissing Dylan good-night on the front porch. She couldn't allow herself to think about whether her outing with Logan tomorrow would end in a kiss. It was enough to acknowledge that he'd asked her on a date, and she'd accepted, and it felt like the best decision she'd made in a long time.

Logan rested his booted feet on the pavement as he parked the motorcycle and shut off the engine. He'd already taken the long way to get here, but he wished he could have stretched out the ride a little longer. Having Caroline riding behind him with her arms draped around his waist had been as close to a perfect moment as he could remember.

But her hands fell away then, and she scooted back from him. Logan climbed off the bike, setting the kickstand, and he helped her down. Though she was the one who'd been nervous all day at the bakery, always fidgeting and avoiding looking at him, he suddenly had misgivings. He'd all but browbeaten her into going out with him last night, and now he wondered if he should have pushed so hard.

Maybe she had been right: maybe they should have thought this through before they made the leap to going on a date. Even if they'd been wise enough not to tell their families about their plans today, he had no illusions that this would be an average first date. No matter what happened today, things between Caroline and him would be different.

"That was amazing!" Caroline yanked off her helmet and finger-combed through her hair that she'd tied back but was still hopelessly tangled. "I've never felt anything so wild and freeing. Why didn't you talk me into taking a ride sooner?"

He grinned at her as he removed his helmet and sat it on the bike. "I wasn't sure I would be able to get you on the bike *this time*. I thought you were going to have a panic attack."

"Well, I did ride it, didn't I?"

"Yes, you did. And you even learned to lean with me in the turns." He rubbed the back of his head. "It might be a few days before my head recovers from you banging into me all the time with your helmet, but otherwise, it was a great ride."

Caroline gave him a mean look, but when she grinned, Logan could finally relax. This wasn't going to be one of those awkward first dates, where they walked on eggshells around each other until they got sick of the misery and went home. It was just another outing with his friend; only the setting had changed. He would worry about any changes in titles later.

As Caroline took a few steps away from the parking lot, Logan waited to hear her reaction to the scenery. He'd never brought a date here before, and he didn't want to examine why it was the first place he'd thought to bring Caroline. Had he been saving it for her?

"I didn't want the ride to end," she said and then gasped. "Oh, my, Logan. This is so beautiful. This is that place you were talking about, isn't it?"

He crossed the lot until he was standing a few steps behind her. The scene had always been amazing, but it was perfect now with Caroline in the center of it.

She turned back to him. "This is where you went on that date with a place rather than a person."

"You remember me saying that?" He stepped next to her and watched her as she stared out into the open space.

"I remember all the things you say." Her gaze flitted his way, but then she turned back to the lookout. "I kept wondering that day about the beautiful woman you had to be out with."

"Were you jealous?"

She didn't look at him or answer, but a pretty pink flush spread on her cheeks.

"Well, *she* was a looker, wasn't she?" He waited to catch her eye and then gestured to the expanse before them.

Logan returned to the motorcycle and opened one of the fringed saddlebags, pulling out a small picnic blanket. From the second saddlebag, he withdrew a collapsible cooler with two plastic-bottled sodas and a couple of sandwiches stuffed inside. He tucked the blanket under his arm and balanced the rest of the items in his arms before starting back to her.

"You thought of everything."

"Peanut butter and jelly. It's not fancy, but we won't starve."

"Beggars can't be choosers. I'm too hungry and too thirsty to get picky."

When he reached her, she pulled the blanket from beneath his arm and spread it on a shady spot near the drop-off. After she settled on it, she reached up, letting him hand the rest of the items down to her.

He took a seat next to her and pointed to the plastic bottles of soda. "I would open those carefully. They took a good shaking on the drive over here."

Caroline lifted the bottle and glanced at the bubbles settling on top of the dark cola. "Maybe I'm not so thirsty after all."

"Come on. You have to take a risk once in a while." He picked up one of the bottles and carefully loosened the cap just a little. When the liquid fizzed, he tightened the lid again. After waiting a few seconds longer, he opened the bottle completely and handed it Caroline.

"Thanks."

Logan started the same process with the second bottle, but the moment he loosened the lid, its liquid contents started spraying like a fire hose. Jumping up, he carried the spraying bottle away from the blanket and tightened the lid, but not before a quarter of the cola had sprayed over his hands and shirt.

He set the bottle on the ground and then stared down at his hands, watching the liquid drip off his fingers. "Well…that happened."

She looked up from where she'd been removing her hiking boots and socks and shook her head. "I think risks are overrated."

"Probably."

He started back for the motorcycle and pulled one last item from the saddlebag: a flat container of wet wipes. "These come in handy sometimes."

Caroline hurried over to help him clean up the mess, and soon they were seated back on the blanket, munching on peanut butter sandwiches and drinking what was left of the sodas. When they were finished, Logan stretched out his legs and rested back on his elbows.

Sitting barefoot and chewing on a blade of grass, Caroline looked more like a back-to-nature gal than a high-powered executive, even one on a hiatus. As she stared out at the same incredible backdrop where he'd often contemplated his life, he couldn't help but wonder if she saw the same things he'd seen, if she'd felt as small and insignificant as he'd felt.

"So you come here to hang out alone for your dates?" she asked finally.

"Mostly I come here to pray. There's just something about being out here surrounded by God's creations."

"It's like your church, right? Like in the Old Testament how Joseph felt close to God when he was out in the field with his flock of sheep."

"I guess it's the same, except that nobody's going to give me a coat of many colors." Though he'd been staring out over the drop-off as he removed his riding boots, Logan turned back to her. "I really do feel closer to God here than I do anywhere else."

"You, Logan Warren, never fail to surprise me."

"Why this time? Because I come out here to pray?"

"No. Because you find the time to come here for private meditation, *and* you go to church every Sunday. Before I came back to Markston, I couldn't tell you the last time I went to church." She tapped her head. "Oh. I remember. Christmas Eve. Back in Markston."

"You couldn't help it. You worked on Sundays, right?"

"I could have found the time to attend services if I'd really wanted to."

"So maybe God used Mom's stroke to speak to both of us in some way."

She seemed to consider what he'd said before she finally nodded. "Wait. What was He trying to show you?"

"He probably wanted me to honor my mother a little more and stop aggravating her by being late to church." At her frown over his joke, he added, "Okay, I think God wanted me to get my priorities straight."

"That makes two of us."

"So how has it been getting back into the church habit since you've been in Markston?"

"It's okay, if you enjoy believing that every one of Reverend Boggs's sermons was written expressly for you."

"I always thought the good reverend wrote all of his messages for me as if I had a target on my head."

They shared a laugh, and then both quieted as they continued to stare into the open space. Logan didn't even mind the lull in the conversation. It felt so good just being there with Caroline, spending time with her in this special space. He hadn't expected her to understand why this place was so important to him, but she had. He wasn't used to anyone getting him that way. He wasn't used to *wanting* someone to know him, either, but for the first time he really wanted that. In a strange way, it seemed as if she already did know him.

Logan was falling in love with Caroline Scott. Though the realization struck him like a blow to the gut, he realized now that the possibility of it had played just outside the reach of his thoughts for days. He didn't know when she'd become more than a friend to him, when caring about her had taken the leap to not being able to imagine life without her, but he couldn't deny the changes.

Even knowing it, though, Logan wasn't sure what he should do about it. He sensed that Caroline had feelings for him, too, but was she ready to admit it? Would she ever be when she could continue to use stories about their shared history and their age difference to distance them? It wasn't wise to risk his heart this way. He was a heartbreak waiting to happen.

He couldn't help himself, though, not with the

possibility of a future with Caroline within his reach. Despite the risk, despite the possible pain, despite everything, he would go beyond standing on the cliff's edge and letting the possibility take him. No, this situation called for a determined leap, and he was ready to take it.

Chapter Twelve

"I'm ready to tell you now."

Caroline had blurted the words before she had the chance to rethink them, but the surprised look on Logan's face made her wonder about her timing. She'd been so nervous about coming here today, wondering if it had been a mistake going on her first date in years with a man who specialized in only first dates.

But she'd felt so comfortable with him that she'd thought it might be the best time to share her story. Maybe there would never be a good time.

"Wait," she said. "Were you about to say something? We can talk about this later."

"Oooh, no," he said, his expression transforming to a grin. "I've waited this long to hear your story. I'm not going to let you back out of it now."

He turned to face her and folded his legs into an uncomfortable-looking crisscross position. "Okay. Spill."

"You make it sound so easy."

But it wasn't, even if she really did want to tell him. Even if he was the first person she'd ever wanted to tell.

With effort, she straightened her shoulders and forced herself to turn and face him. She folded her legs like his.

"It was the biggest failure of my life." She paused, lifting and lowering her shoulders. "Okay, until I got the pink slip."

"Which is a whole other subject, so…"

"Did I ever tell you that you're a pushy person?"

"Hmm." He leaned his elbow on his leg and rested his chin on his fist in a contemplative pose. "I don't think so, but have I ever told you that you're stalling?"

Caroline crossed her arms but then shook them out again and planted her palms on her thighs. "I was nineteen. His name was Kevin. We were both business majors, both driven and ambitious, with these king-sized dreams and goals that we shared in common."

"Sounds romantic. Like a match made…on Wall Street." He chuckled.

"Do you want to hear this or not?"

Instead of answering, he moved his hand in a circular motion to signal for her to continue.

"It was one of those whirlwind romances. Not like me at all. He proposed, and I accepted." She shook her head at the memory, hating any reminder that she could have been so naive. "Then before I'd even figured out how to tell my parents, it was over."

An unreadable expression covered Logan's face, and he looked away for a few seconds before finally turning back. "What happened?"

"A couple of things, really. First, he told me that after we were married, he didn't want me to work."

"For you, that must have been like asking you not to breathe."

Caroline's gaze connected with his and held. He wasn't laughing at her as she'd first suspected. He just *knew* her. She wondered now if he was the only person who ever had.

"Yeah," she said, lowering her gaze to the blanket.

"As if that wasn't enough, you said there were a couple of things. What else happened?"

"After I said I couldn't believe he would ask me to give up my dreams for his, Kevin said we never would have worked out, anyway. Then he told me about his other girlfriend. I kind of objected to her, too."

"What a complete idiot! How could he ever even think about—" Logan stopped himself and looked up at her sheepishly. "Sorry. Go on."

Caroline couldn't help grinning at him. "I felt the same way, only I realized I was the idiot for taking a chance like that. Anyway, thanks for being on my side."

"Always."

When she glanced up at him, his gaze was warmer even than the sun on her face. Strange, but she didn't think he was talking about the show of support he'd just given her, and stranger than that, she was glad.

"So, that's it?" he asked her. "I thought this story was going to be really ugly."

"Yes, that's it. Don't you think that's bad enough?"

Instead of making another joke, Logan nodded. "It was bad enough to keep you from ever dating after that."

"I told you that it was more about me being career-focused and—" She stopped when his expression told her he didn't believe her. The words didn't even ring true in her ears anymore.

He watched her for several long seconds. "Were there no signs that you weren't the only woman in his life?"

"In retrospect, sure. Calls from his 'study partner.' Nights when he was supposed to be at his off-campus job, but he never had any money." She reached off the blanket and started plucking handfuls of grass, letting it fall back to the earth.

"It's much easier to analyze our lives in the rearview mirror than to see any of it with the headlights," Logan said with a shrug.

"Why, Logan Warren, that's awfully profound."

"I've had a lot of time for profound thoughts on afternoons up here at the lookout."

"So, what other profound thoughts have you had here in this place that belongs on a postcard?"

"Just one more."

"Then it has to be a good one. What is it?"

"You're not living if you're not taking any chances."

"Oh." She cleared her throat. "Is that thought specifically for me or a general worldview?"

She would need to tell him soon that she was taking a chance this coming week in Chicago when she interviewed for that new position, but somehow now didn't seem like the time to tell him. She'd been reluctant to tell him all week.

"If the shoe fits." He must have expected her to argue because he held up his hand before she had the chance. "It fits me, too, Caroline."

"What do you mean it fits you?"

He'd been serious when he'd said it, but suddenly he grinned. "I don't know whether I can take the risk of going for a hike with a novice outdoorswoman like you."

"Is that a challenge? You know I can't turn down a challenge." She glanced over at the pair of old hiking boots of Haley's that she'd worn with her shorts and T-shirt today. "I have my boots so I'm equipped for a hike. At least a short one."

"Then it's a challenge." He wore a pained expression as he unfolded his legs and reached for his boots.

Caroline recognized a dodged question when she heard one, but his hedge let her off the hook as well, so she didn't push the subject. She slipped back on her socks and boots and started lacing up the shoestrings. "You're sure you can handle hiking with me?"

"My riding boots will make it rough, but remember, we're in my territory now."

Finished with his boots first, Logan reached out his right hand to her left and helped her to her feet. But when she was standing next to him, he didn't release her. Instead he shifted his hand, and suddenly their fingers were laced together.

For a few seconds, Caroline could only stare down at their hands, marveling at how right it felt for them to be holding hands, how safe she felt just being near him. Still, it took all the courage she could muster to look up at him.

"Nice trick." Her titter gave away her nervousness, but she couldn't help it. She'd never been an expert at dating, and now she was out of practice, too.

"If you say something about my skills as Logan-the-lady-killer, this hike is going to move from beginning to advanced level in a heartbeat." He took a step forward and tugged so that she came with him.

"I didn't say anything."

"Good." He glanced sidelong at her and then down at their hands. "This is okay, then?"

She nodded instead of answering because it not only was more than okay, it was also as close to perfect as anything she'd ever experienced and she couldn't say anything without sounding downright giddy.

He led her across the parking lot to a paved hiking trail. "Because none of this is easy."

"What isn't easy? The trail?" She waited, but he didn't answer as they continued farther down the trail.

"With you," he said finally.

"Me?" The squeak in her voice humiliated her. At least he couldn't hear the way her pulse pounded in her ears.

"I've been on hundreds of dates, but it's different with you." He shrugged. "Like it's the first time I've done this or something."

"Oh." Her thoughts raced with questions she couldn't ask. Did it feel different to him because it was the first time he'd gone on a date with a Scott sister? Or was it something more than that? Did she want it to be more than that when time was ticking down for her return to Chicago? When the opportunities she had long been waiting for had finally been lining up for her? More surprising than any of the other questions, would she be crushed if there weren't something significant between them?

But Logan gave no hints as they passed trees and brush, his gaze pausing on two chipmunks chasing each other across the path.

"Are you really going to leave me hanging after saying something like that?"

He didn't look at her, but the side of his mouth lifted. "That isn't fair, is it?"

"No. It's not, and I think you should—"

"I never take chances," he blurted to interrupt her. "That's what I meant about the situation fitting me, too. I was always more willing to go on one hundred first dates than to risk the possibility of a second one."

"Are you serious?" Caroline stopped quickly and yanked on his hand so Logan stopped with her. He released her hand, and immediately her skin felt cold from the loss of his touch. But she couldn't believe what she'd heard. After all the things she'd told herself to set them apart, was it possible that in relationships at least they shared something as elemental as fear in common? "But you're an expert at this dating business."

"Yes, I am. That's the point." His frustration was palpable as he tilted his head toward the sky, his jaw tight. Finally, he looked back at her. "Look. You know about my dad. You know what he did to the people he was supposed to love."

All of a sudden, everything made sense to her. "This is all about your dad, isn't it? You're not worried about getting hurt. You're more afraid that you'll be like your father. That you'll hurt someone else."

"I don't know," he said with a shrug. "But what if it's true? What if I am my father's son?"

"That's crazy. How could you think that?" She'd always hated what Elliot Warren had done to his sons when he'd deserted them but never more than right now. "The others were wrong to think that as the oldest, Matthew was hurt the most by your father's desertion. If you believe you could be anything like your dad, then I think he hurt you even more. You're nothing like him."

"How can you know that for sure?"

Caroline smiled back at him. "There are probably dozens of ways, but here's just one. If you were like him, you wouldn't care whether or not you hurt someone. You wouldn't have any reason to avoid relationships because other people's feelings wouldn't matter to you."

"Maybe you just don't know me well enough. I could be like that."

"If you believe that, why are you telling me now instead of last night when you insisted that I go out with you? Are you worried that I won't know that I'm just one in your series of first dates? Don't worry. I'm a smart woman. I get it." She held her hands wide to emphasize her point.

Logan shocked her by reaching out to take both of her hands and pull them together. Caroline swallowed, searching for answers in his serious face.

"That's what I'm trying to say, Caroline. You're special. You could never be just another date to me."

Caroline drew in a ragged breath, her pulse pounding like it did after her cycling classes. Had he just said some of the things to her that she daydreamed he would? She knew she should say or do something, but she felt frozen in place.

He must have either recognized her predicament or he was on a roll, because he didn't wait for her to answer. "This is the first time I've ever wanted more than one date with a woman. It's all brand-new, and I'm scared to death." Logan paused, squeezing her hands. "I couldn't bear it if I hurt you."

"But you would never do that." She stared at the ground as she spoke, but once she began, she couldn't seem to stop herself. "Don't you see? You're kind and compassionate and self-sacrificing. Just look at the way you returned to Markston after college, just to be near your mother."

"That's no great feat. I love Markston. I can't ever picture myself living anywhere else."

Caroline shook her head. She wasn't going to let him get away with putting himself down this time, with failing to see himself the way she saw him.

"You didn't hesitate to put your life on hold for your mom after her stroke. And look at how hard you've worked to get past those protective walls I'd built around myself. You would never hurt me because you're... you."

Caroline looked up then, shocked by the flow of words that had been like a dam break. These weren't the words that someone whose presence was temporary at best should have been saying, but she couldn't stop herself from speaking the truth.

Logan stared back at her, his eyes wide, his mouth slack. She couldn't blame him. She'd all but said she loved him on their first date. Did she love him? Could all of these feelings of angst and intensity and surprise mean that she'd fallen in love with Logan Warren? How could she know for sure?

She waited for him to say something—anything—but for several long seconds he stood staring at her, looking every bit as frozen as she had moments before. And then before she had time to process what was going to happen, Logan pulled her closer with their joined hands and lowered his head, taking her mouth with his.

It wasn't a tender first kiss but one of old hurts and emotional need and, finally, like the first spring buds after a harsh winter, healing. He pulled back slightly, dropped her hands and stared down at her, looking as startled as she felt over the kiss.

"I'm sorry. That was not the way I planned to do that. It was supposed to be special and perfect and... But you said all those amazing things and I..."

His vulnerability was so sweet—particularly in the realm of dating—that Caroline couldn't help but smile up at him.

"What are you smiling at?"

"I was just wondering if you would be willing to demonstrate for me how you'd *planned* to do that."

Logan blinked, but then a slow smile spread across his lips. "I could do that."

With slow, careful precision, he lifted his hands to cradle her face. Her eyes fluttered closed in sweet anticipation, and this time when he bent close to her, he pressed his lips to hers in a heart-stoppingly dear and gentle kiss. As Logan continued adoring her with his kisses, brushing his lips over the corners of her mouth, Caroline couldn't help but lift her hands to rest in the baby-fine hair at his nape.

Before she would have preferred it, Logan touched her shoulders and set her back from him. Caroline blinked a few times as the real world came into focus again.

"That was nice," she breathed just above a whisper. She looked up, noticing for the first time that the trees lining the wide trail curled over them, creating an intimate, archlike setting.

Logan took a deep breath and let it whistle out through his teeth. "Too nice."

When he reached up to tuck a loose strand of hair back behind her ear, she pressed her cheek into his hand, and then she turned her head to drop a kiss on his palm.

His eyes widening, Logan drew back his hand and took a step back from her.

"Have mercy on a poor guy who's trying to be a gentleman here," he said when she looked at him, confused.

A lump surprised her by forming in her throat. She'd been kissed before—even if it had been a few years—but never like this, full of promises and joy. No man had ever made her feel more treasured…or more loved.

Was it possible that Logan loved her, too? As soon as the thought crossed her mind, she smiled. *Too.* She did love him. It was as if a part of her had always been missing, and she had found the missing piece in him. Finally, she could admit, at least to herself, what her heart had known all along.

Logan was having a hard time keeping from smiling as he turned his motorcycle out of the state park exit for the drive back to Markston. Only the threat of a June bug getting lodged in his teeth kept him from showing off a toothy grin. He wasn't even the Pollyanna type, yet he found himself wondering if the day could get any better.

The date with Caroline had been like the best destination in the longest journey, like the final bell in a lifetime of speed dating. Not that the date hadn't been nerve-racking. That it mattered to him this time made all the difference.

He still couldn't believe he'd pulled her to him and kissed her like that. He'd just been marveling at the things she'd said and how she saw right through him, and then suddenly he was holding her in his arms. If she'd ever thought of him as the suave ladies' man, she couldn't believe that anymore after that awkward move.

At least she'd given him a second chance, so they could share a perfect *second* kiss. It had felt so right holding Caroline in that incredible outdoor setting, the breeze lifting strands of her hair.

Though it had taken all his strength to set her away from him, he was glad he'd been able to show her that she was precious. She was like an answer to a prayer request he'd never thought to make.

Even now, as Caroline sat on the motorcycle behind him, her arms wrapped around his waist, Logan couldn't get over how great he felt just being near her. Her support made him feel strong enough to take on the world. She expected the best from him and believed he could give it. She made him want to be a better man.

"Thank you, God," he said in a low voice, aware that the wind rushing at them would keep Caroline from hearing.

But when they reached an intersection, Caroline tapped the back of his helmet with hers. "Did you say something?" she called out over the roar of the motor.

Turning his head to the side, he grinned. "Never mind."

Too soon they were back in the bakery parking lot so that Caroline could pick up her car. Logan climbed off the motorcycle when she did and removed his helmet, hoping to delay her for a few more minutes. If it wouldn't have made him sound needy, he would have continued making excuses for her to stay until after midnight.

"I had a really nice time, Logan. Even if I had to earn my lunch by hiking through the woods." She paused and started trying to smooth out her tangles. "And I'm pretty sure this is a bug." She indicated a spot of hair just past her ear.

He leaned close and examined her hair. "It's not a—"

But her laugh stopped him. "Funny. I had a great time, too."

Caroline glanced at his motorcycle and then over at her car. She didn't fidget the way she did when she was nervous, but she clearly recognized that it was time for them to go. Time for this date was running out.

"Do you want to do something again tomorrow after church?" He was doing the unthinkable, but he couldn't help it. He'd never wanted a second date before, and yet he couldn't imagine not having a second one this time. Or a third. Or a fourth. "Maybe we could fit something in between lunch at your mom's and the visit to the rehab center."

"I'd like that."

"Me, too." They exchanged a look that made him want to kiss her all over again. "But there's something we need to figure out first. How much should we tell our families?"

"You mean with the wedding coming up next week? Do you think we should keep this—whatever *this* is—to ourselves so we don't take anyone's thunder?"

He nodded. Only after she'd asked those reasonable questions and disappointment settled inside him did Logan realize how much he'd hoped Caroline would want to go public with their budding relationship. Of course, she was right about everything, even that their relationship wasn't defined enough yet to share, but part of him had hoped she would want to shout it from the rooftops as he was tempted to do. "You're right. We should wait."

Caroline watched him for several seconds. "Nah."

"What?"

"We might turn a few heads at church tomorrow, but everyone will get over it. Mom will be especially surprised since she didn't lift a finger for this matchup. By the time the wedding comes, we'll be old news." Her gaze narrowed. "You will be my date to the wedding, won't you?"

"It'd be great." Logan hated that his pulse picked up, but he couldn't help it, not when there was a chance that she might feel as strongly as he did. He would have told her he loved her, but he figured it would sound desperate if he told her before their second date.

"It will be a relief, too. My sisters were starting to get some ideas about setting me up at the wedding." She tapped her first two fingers together to imitate cutting with scissors. "This will cut them off at the knees."

"It sure will."

Logan tried to keep the disappointment from his voice and was relieved when she missed it. He wanted to be more to her than just her way of avoiding someone's matchmaking attempts. After all those things she'd said earlier, he had to believe that he was, but he had to tread carefully. He couldn't push her for any commitment too fast, or he might scare her away.

"So, I'll pick you up before services tomorrow."

"Don't you just want to meet there?"

Logan shook his head. It was important to him that they made the statement of arriving to church as a couple. "Be ready. Bright and early."

She seemed to consider for a few seconds, and then her lips lifted. "Okay, I'll be ready. Early."

Stepping close to him, Caroline lifted on her tiptoes and pressed a gentle kiss to his lips. Then with a bashful grin, she turned away and headed to her car.

Logan couldn't stop smiling as he watched her pull from the lot. Everything was going to fine, he was suddenly certain. He couldn't wait to walk into church tomorrow and show his brothers that he, too, had found someone to love. That she just happened to be a Scott sister was a bonus.

He recognized that Caroline was nervous about making that appearance, but he would ease all of her worries. He would do everything in his power to assure her that she'd made the right decision in taking a chance on him.

Chapter Thirteen

Caroline rearranged herself again in the pew, crossing and uncrossing her legs, the sense of foreboding so strong that she couldn't sit still. She'd realized that this morning's service would be different, but she hadn't expected this strange feeling that something was wrong.

Seated next to her, Logan squeezed her hand. "You okay? They'll stop staring before too long. They weren't even all that shocked when we walked in."

He gestured down the pew to Jenna and Haley, who were trading off taking surreptitious looks at them and then putting their heads together to whisper. Lizzie wasn't even trying to hide that she was staring and kept trying to sneak to the opposite end of the pew to reach them, but Haley wouldn't let go of her hand.

"The only way they would have been more shocked was if I showed up at church holding hands with a little green Martian," Caroline told him.

"You see? It definitely could have been worse, then." He reached over to pat their joined hands with his free one.

"Dylan didn't seem surprised."

"He wasn't. He figured everything out at the barbecue the other day."

"Why? We weren't together that day." She started to pull away from him, but he only held her hand between both of his.

"He saw the way I looked at you."

Automatically, her gaze sought out his, and her heart squeezed in her chest. Anyone seeing the way Logan Warren looked at her, or the way she looked at him for that matter, would have recognized their chemistry. "Oh. He doesn't seem all that pleased."

"He warned me to be careful." Logan brushed his shoulder against hers. "He's worried you'll break my heart."

She shook her head, frowning. Shifting again, she couldn't help looking back to the doors separating the sanctuary from the vestibule.

"I was sure Mom would have been here by now. She's never late."

"Unlike me?" He grinned as he flipped open his cell phone and checked the time. "She still has a few minutes. She'll be rushing in here in no time."

"We should have brought her when you picked me up."

True to his word, Logan had arrived early to give her a ride, not quite as early as when Dylan had picked up Jenna but before her mother had been ready for church.

"She told us to go ahead, that she'd catch up with us here," he said.

Caroline shrugged. "She probably needed time to get over the shock of seeing us together."

"Maybe."

He chuckled but was checking the door frequently himself. Was he starting to worry that something might be wrong, too? Her mother had seemed fine when they'd left, but then Logan and his brothers had never expected their mother to have a stroke, either.

Lizzie must have escaped from Haley's hold because she sidled down the pew and sat next to them. Caroline released Logan's hand but not soon enough for the child to miss it.

"Uncle Logan and Aunt Caroline, are you going to get married like Aunt Jenna and Uncle Dylan?"

Caroline coughed into her hand, so Logan answered for the both of them.

"Not anytime soon, anyway, munchkin." He reached over and tugged one of her pigtails.

Caroline's breath caught. *Not soon* suggested that he thought it could happen sometime. That part of her was excited at the prospect instead of terrified the way she should have been made her nervous. Their relationship was moving too fast.

Seeming satisfied with his answer, Lizzie scooted back down the pew to her mother. Haley looked over at them apologetically and then turned to glance at the back door.

The prelude music was already playing. Usually, Matthew already would have been seated on his music minister's bench by now. Even Dylan and Jenna had stopped whispering and were watching the door. Instead of Matthew, Reverend Boggs came through it, hurrying toward the podium. When he reached it, he stepped right to the lectern and motioned for the organist to stop playing.

"Fellow believers, I have some sad news for you this morning," he began. "I received a call…"

Caroline sat frozen in her seat. She didn't hear whatever else the minister said, but she didn't need to hear to know that it had something to do with her family and that it was something awful. Memories of her father's death stole into her thoughts, causing a lump to form in her throat.

"Over there, Caroline," Logan whispered.

He brushed her side with his elbow and then indicated the other end of the pew with a tilt of his head. Standing at the end of the pew was Matthew, his expression the practiced blank look that the clergy used in times of bereavement. Immediately, Caroline's whole body went cold.

Matthew was helping his wife to her feet, his daughter already clinging to Haley's leg. Matthew signaled for the others to follow and then started up the aisle to the exit. Dylan and Jenna slid out behind him, and Caroline followed them with Logan coming last. Once they all reached the vestibule and the door closed behind them, Matthew turned to face the others.

"What is it, Matthew?" Haley asked, her cheeks ruddy from the excitement.

"Tell us," Caroline said.

"Will you say something already?" Logan insisted.

Matthew held up his hands to stop the barrage. "It's Mom. She had several mini-strokes overnight. They took her from the rehab center back to Markston Area Regional by ambulance." He glanced at his wife and her sisters. "Your mom's there with her now."

"Oh, no," Caroline said as some of the others gasped. Her heart ached for Logan's mother, who'd been making such wonderful progress until now, as much as for her own mother, who had to be in agony watching her friend suffering.

"What does all of this mean?" Logan asked for all of them.

"Often mini-strokes precede a major stroke. If Mom has another one, her doctors are worried she won't—"

Matthew stopped as his gaze lowered to Lizzie, who looked up at him with worry clouding her eyes. She had to be the only one in the room who didn't realize that his next word would be *survive.*

"Daddy, is Grammy going to be okay?"

"We sure hope so, sweetheart." He bent and wrapped his arm around his daughter's shoulders. "The doctors are doing everything they can to make sure she is, but we're going to do something even more important."

"What?" she wanted to know.

"We're going to pray." With his hand, he indicated the windows that separated the sanctuary from the entry area. "Just like so many of our friends are praying in there."

Matthew held out both of his hands, and soon their families were joined in a circle of prayer.

"Lord, please rest Your loving hand on Your child, Amy," Matthew prayed. "Comfort her and give her peace. We're asking for a miracle, Lord, if it is Your will."

"Amen," they all chorused.

Most of them released hands, but Matthew and Haley continued to cling to each other, as did Jenna and Dylan. As she felt the squeeze, Caroline realized that Logan was still holding her hand, as well.

She should have found comfort in the fact that she

and Logan could support each other just as their siblings were sustaining each other. Instead, she felt a strange temptation to yank her hand away and run. She shook away the impulse—Logan needed her and she would be there for him—but a sense of dread clung to her with piercing claws.

Was she the only one who recognized that no matter what happened today, everything had changed? Even if God performed a miracle and the doctors were able to stabilize Mrs. Warren, she would probably never be able to return to her job at the bakery. Another massive stroke would always be a possibility on the horizon, a risk to Mrs. Warren's health that her sons wouldn't want to take by allowing her to return to work.

She was in too deep, Caroline realized suddenly. She'd allowed this relationship with Logan to blossom when it had no place to grow, as she would be returning to her real life. How could she tell him that he was going to get stuck running the business indefinitely and that, just when he needed her, she would be deserting him just like his father had?

The waiting room at Markston Area Regional Hospital looked like a Warren-Scott family reunion, yet no one was laughing or even smiling. Lunchtime had come and gone, and they were all still there, talking in hushed voices, praying and waiting for any word from the doctors who'd been frustratingly silent so far.

Logan wondered why the doctors couldn't tell them something. Anything. Even during those measly fifteen minutes when he and Matthew had been allowed to sit with his mother in ICU, she'd been sedated, so they hadn't learned anything new about her condition.

Shoving a hand back through his hair, Logan rested his head on the back of the chair where he'd tossed his suit jacket and tie when he couldn't bear to be in them anymore. He refused to believe his mother wouldn't be all right. This was just a minor setback. It had to be.

He had to trust that God would bring her back to all of these people who loved her. But because it wasn't always so easy to believe, Logan squeezed his eyes shut, battling emotions that came with his fear. When he opened his eyes, he reached for the cup on the table next to him and took a sip of coffee that had been lousy when it was hot and unbearable now that it was tepid.

He wished Caroline were still beside him as she'd been the first hour or so, but she'd joined her mother and Dylan and Jenna as they'd been trying to decide what to do about the wedding. The four of them had been crowded around that table in the corner for what seemed like forever.

"Want me to go get more of that?"

As Logan looked up, Matthew, who'd suddenly stepped in front of him, was pointing at the cup of dark liquid.

"Only if you're trying to poison me."

"A large cup, then?"

Logan didn't have the energy to smile at his brother's attempt at humor. Leaning forward in the chair, he covered his face with his hands and smoothed his fingers across the headache forming behind his eyebrows. "Don't worry about me. I'd be more concerned about your wife. She looked pretty upset earlier."

"She told me to stop hovering and to go find something to do," Matthew said with a shrug.

"Got to give Haley credit. She keeps you in line."

Logan almost smiled this time as he glanced over at Haley, who was sitting with her legs propped up on an office-furniture-style love seat and with a pillow tucked behind her back. On the seat opposite hers, Lizzie napped beneath a hospital blanket that one of the nurses had been kind enough to share.

"She was having some Braxton Hicks contractions, but they've stopped now. Those are the practice kind. She said it was probably from getting herself so worked up earlier." Matthew glanced back at her, not appearing convinced that all was well.

"Don't worry," Logan said. "She'll be fine. The baby, too."

Logan could understand his brother's need to be overprotective of his wife. He could only imagine what a mother hen he would be if Caroline were his wife and she were pregnant with his child. At the thought, he grinned. He was having a difficult enough time trying not to stare at her right now and she was only across the room.

"What are you grinning at?"

"Oh. Sorry." He wiped the expression from his face. "I know there's no reason to smile today."

"It depends on whether or not you believe that God answers prayer."

Because Logan had been watching their family and friends at the table again, it took a few seconds for his brother's words to sink in. He looked back to Matthew.

"Of course I believe—"

Before he could get the retort out, his brother reached over and patted him on the shoulder. "I know you do. I just thought we both could use a reminder. Anyway,

Mom would never want us to stop smiling, no matter what. Particularly those of us who happen to be in love."

Matthew glanced over at Caroline and grinned as he turned back to Logan. "Now that one is a surprise. I know Mom will be surprised."

Glancing sidelong at him, Logan considered denying it, but finally he nodded. "It caught us off guard, too. We're the only ones Mom and Mrs. Scott didn't try to push together."

"Has my mother-in-law said anything to you two yet?"

Logan shook his head. "She didn't have time before church, and then she's been—" he paused to glance at Mrs. Scott as she led the conversation in the corner "—preoccupied since we've been here."

Either that or she disagreed so vehemently with the choices that Caroline and Logan had made that she couldn't speak to either of them about it yet.

"So you and Caroline have both made—" Matthew paused as if searching for the right word "—declarations?"

Logan shook his head. "It's too new. Brand-new." He blew out a frustrated breath. "I have lousy timing."

"Don't we all?" Matthew patted his shoulder again. "But isn't it great that our Lord's timing is perfect?"

With a grin, Matthew continued into the vending area in search of more of that lousy coffee.

After Logan leaned back in his chair again, Caroline came over and sat next to him. He was relieved that she'd come to him, especially since she'd been acting strangely ever since they'd heard the bad news at church. She hadn't even touched him since they'd left the church though he really would have liked to hold her hand as they waited here. Everyone reacted to worry differently, but he was beginning to wonder if her odd distance might be something that should concern him more.

"Well, what did they decide?"

"Jenna and Dylan are going to postpone the wedding," Caroline told him. "They know your mom wouldn't be happy about that decision, but they want their wedding to be a joyous occasion, and they don't think they can be in a festive mood until they know she's on the mend."

"Yeah, I get that. I wouldn't have been in the mood to turn cartwheels next week as best man, either."

"Well, obviously, since you were planning to do cartwheels at the ceremony—" she paused to indicate the crowded waiting room with a sweep of her arm "—before all of this."

She was trying to make him laugh, and he loved her even more for that. "Well, I guess your family knows better than anybody how to dismantle a wedding."

"It does give Mom something to do while she waits on word about Mrs. Warren's condition," she said.

Jenna had crossed the room to Logan and Caroline in time to hear the last few comments. "We're not *canceling* it, Logan. Just *postponing* it."

"Thanks for the reminder," Haley said with a tight chuckle.

"You kidding?" Matthew said as he returned, balancing a steaming cup of liquid. "That canceled wedding was the best thing that ever happened to me."

"You can say that again, buddy," Dylan piped.

Trina came to sit next to Haley, who had shifted so her knees were just below her rounded belly. "I know someone else who's happy that wedding never took place." She reached over and brushed back Haley's spiky hair before turning back to Dylan and Jenna. "But this particular wedding will happen when the time is right."

"Yeah, you two, it's going to be a great wedding whenever you reschedule it," Logan added.

The nurse appeared in the doorway of the waiting room, signaling that two of his mother's visitors could take their fifteen-minute visit for the hour. As they'd all planned, Dylan and Jenna took this shift, following the nurse back through the double doors.

The doors had barely closed behind them when Haley let out a strangled cry. In the short time it took Mrs. Scott to turn back to her youngest daughter, Caroline and Matthew were already kneeling next to her.

"Honey, you said you're okay. You're not okay." Matthew's voice rose in pitch with each word he spoke.

"I'm fine." Haley's voice sounded strained, and she grimaced as she spoke.

"Is it the baby?" Caroline asked, taking hold of her hand. "You've just had too much excitement. It can't be good for you or for the baby."

Caroline turned to Matthew. "Maybe you should take Haley and Lizzie home. There's nothing you can do here, and we'll call you as soon as we know—"

Trina put her hand on Caroline's arm to interrupt her. "Caroline, she's not going anywhere."

"Really," Haley insisted. "I'm okay."

But her mother would have none of it. "Could someone get a nurse in here?" She indicated with her hand that she'd selected Logan as the *someone*. "Go tell her Haley might be in labor."

Chapter Fourteen

Caroline was so exhausted that she didn't even object when Logan walked her up the steps of her mother's house, took the keys from her hands and unlocked the door. She wished he hadn't followed her inside, but she was too tired to challenge that, either. Too many things had happened today for her to consider bringing up the subject that they needed to discuss. She would put it off until tomorrow if he would only let her.

"Why don't you have a seat in the family room. I'll make us some tea." Logan didn't wait for an answer before he started toward the kitchen.

Caroline followed him down the hall until he made a right turn into the kitchen, leaving her to turn the opposite direction into the family room. The rooms were close enough that they still could hold a conversation without raising their voices, even as she collapsed on the sofa and he banged around in the cabinets, looking for a teakettle.

"Didn't you get enough caffeine at the hospital?"

"Yeah. I'm wired now, so I could use some herbal tea

to settle my mind." He came to the doorway and looked out at her.

"Are you going to make some for Dylan and Jenna?"

He tilted his head and looked at her strangely. "Don't you remember? Jenna volunteered to spend the night with Lizzie at Matthew and Haley's, so Matthew could stay at the hospital. Dylan said he would bring home your mother, but he's probably still trying to convince her to leave the hospital."

"Oh. Right. I knew all that."

The kettle whistled, so Logan turned back to the stove. After more cabinet banging, he emerged from the kitchen carrying two steaming mugs. He waited as she sat up to accept one, and then he handed it to her.

"Thanks."

"You look like you could use this, too." He watched her as he took a seat next to her. "You've been stressed out all day."

Caroline bristled under his observation. "Well, it's been a stressful day."

"That it has," he said with a chuckle that bore no real humor. "Who knew that so much could happen at once?"

"A chain reaction of events." She blew on the steam at the rim of her cup and took a sip. As the warm liquid slid down her throat, she felt calm for the first time all day. "Haley's OB said the stress brought on her premature labor."

"At least the medication stopped it, for tonight anyway." Logan's jaw flexed as if he were thinking darker thoughts. "You heard what the doctor said. Just because they stopped it tonight doesn't mean that the whole thing won't start up again tomorrow."

"It's not that early, anyway. It's less than four weeks until her due date," Caroline reminded him. "Haley's going to hate it if they put her on bed rest all the way until the delivery."

Caroline could already picture her youngest sister going stir-crazy sitting in bed and waiting for others to care for her.

"But she'll do what she has to do to protect her baby." Logan balanced the cup on his knee but didn't drink any. "My nephew needs as much time to develop as he can get."

"Nephew?" Her senses might have been off today, but she didn't miss that one.

"Oops. I wasn't supposed to say that." He pinched his nose and shook his head. "I guess I'm exhausted, too, if I just spilled the beans. Matthew wanted to know the baby's gender, but Haley didn't. He had to tell someone."

"Don't worry. I'm not going to tell."

He nodded, appearing grateful. "You only got in to see Mom one time today, didn't you?"

"I thought it was more important that you three guys kept getting in. She needs to know that her sons are there for her." Caroline felt strangely relieved that they'd stayed on these "light" topics instead of delving into deeper things. She wasn't ready to talk about those other things, anyway. Wasn't sure yet what to say.

"Mom needs support from all of us."

"I know that. It's just that there was only limited visitation time tonight, and I thought the three of you should get more of it than the rest of us."

Logan nodded and then he took a sip of his tea, set the cup on a coaster and turned back to her. "Caroline, would you please tell me what's going on?"

"I don't know what you mean," she said to stall because she didn't know how to answer his question. Setting her cup on the side table, she clasped her hands in her lap. It was all she could do not to wring them.

"You've been acting strangely ever since Matthew gave us the bad news at church."

"As I said, it's been a stressful day."

He reached out and covered her clasped hands. Caroline stared down at her hands, needing the warmth and comfort that his provided, yet preparing herself for the loss of their touch. Misunderstanding her dilemma, he pulled his hand away, leaving her skin cold.

"So stressful that you haven't been able to bring yourself to touch me all afternoon?"

Caroline stared at her lap again. She'd wanted to reach out to him all day, to feel the protection of having his strong arm to steady her, but then she'd thought about why they were at the hospital, and she'd felt frozen.

"Everything's just too confusing," she said finally. "It's all happening at once. There's too much."

"Just tell me, Caroline, what's going on?"

"Maybe we stepped forward too fast. Maybe we should have thought it through before we let things change between us. Before we let ourselves think—" She shook her head, trying to rid her mind of the things she'd thought, the things that would never be.

His jaw was tight, but he only nodded. "Now don't stop there. You'd better tell me all of it."

"Markston is part of who you are. You thrive here.

You have your family and history here and even a job that fits you and makes you happy."

"That's true." He drew his eyebrows together, clearly not getting it.

"I was born here, but Markston is not who I am," she said, explaining what should have been obvious to him. "We're opposites in a lot of ways."

"These are not new revelations, Caroline. We knew these things about each other yesterday at the park." His look was so intense that he seemed to see right through her. "Don't you remember it? When we were kissing."

"I remember." And she probably would be able to recall every detail of that afternoon for the rest of her life.

"Then what is this about?"

"Your mom," she said in a burst of frustration. "Am I the only one who recognizes that Mrs. Warren might never come back to Amy's Elite Treats?"

Logan's head jerked back as if she'd slapped him instead of just injuring him with her words. "Don't say that." He shook his head as if to force away the possibility that she was right. "You know how stubborn she is. If she wants to come back, she'll be coming back."

"I know how stubborn *you* are." She'd surprised herself by saying it, but because she couldn't take it back, she pressed forward, determined to say the rest. "No matter how many times I've tried to bring it up the possibility that she won't be able to work again, you've put me off. Did you think that by ignoring it, the problem would just go away?"

The look he gave her suggested that had been exactly what he'd thought, but he shook his head.

"I haven't *ignored* anything. I've been at the bakery

every day except Sundays. I've clocked more hours than even you to make sure it keeps going."

"But why did you do it?" She held her hands wide to emphasize the point that he wasn't getting. "You've thrown yourself into this business so you could keep it afloat until your mother could return. But you wouldn't allow yourself to think about what you would do if she couldn't come back."

Since Logan was staring at the floor instead of looking at her, she guessed he wouldn't be answering. She hated causing him pain, but he needed to hear these things, and she had to be the one to tell him.

"I know this is difficult, but at some point, your brothers and you are going to have to consider your options for selling the business." She waited for him to look up, but he didn't. "It will be painful, but you'll be able to use the money to help cover your mother's medical bills and rehabilitation costs," she added.

Logan glanced up then, and the fury in his eyes was enough to cause her to shift back in her seat.

"Are you listening to yourself? I can't believe you even suggested it. You're worrying about medical bills when Mom is still in the hospital, still not knowing if another major stroke is just around the corner. You've been with us all day. Can't you try to believe she's going to be okay?"

His words stung, but she tried not to let it show. "Of course I want to believe it. I'm praying for your mother as often as any of you are, but I'm being realistic. It's not personal," she said, shrugging. "It's just business."

He made a scoffing sound. "You know a lot about running a business, Caroline. Probably more than I could learn in a decade. But there's one thing you still don't get, even after losing your last job and after spending all this time at the bakery." He waited until she was looking back at him before he continued. "Business is always personal when it affects you."

Caroline swallowed, his words having hit their mark. Her boss told her it wasn't personal when he'd let her go, too, but it couldn't have felt more personal to her. "You know what I mean," she said.

"I guess I don't. Just like you don't get that for me to give up on the business would be like giving up on Mom ever recovering. I can't give up on her."

"So you see? You're stuck," Caroline said. "If you don't figure out something soon, you'll never go back to the job you love. You'll be left here running the bakery indefinitely."

"It isn't getting stuck with anything when I'm choosing to care for Mom's business for as long as she needs me. It's a choice. What about you?" Suddenly, he stopped and stared at her. "That's it. This isn't about me losing my career at all. It's about you. You're afraid of getting stuck here in Markston with—"

He stopped himself before he said "me," but she heard it as clearly as if he'd shouted it.

"You know that's not it. We both have lives to get back to, and mine happens to be back in Chicago."

"That's where it used to be," he said flatly.

"No, it's still there. My apartment's there. My things and my friends are there. And if everything works out with the interview next week, I'll have what could possibly be another dream job there, too."

"When were you planning to tell me this?"

Caroline blinked as the hurt in his voice filtered through her senses. Anger she'd expected, but she hadn't prepared herself for the hurt. "You know that I've been in a job search ever since I came back to Markston. I couldn't work without an income indefinitely. I just haven't had any solid leads until this one."

"How long have you known about the interview?"

"Just a few days. Really."

"Since before the July Fourth holiday? Since before *yesterday?*"

Caroline coughed into her hand. He was right, of course. He'd deserved the reminder that she was only in Markston a short time before he invested himself in a relationship that was temporary at best.

"I should have told you, but I didn't know anything for certain—I still don't—so I didn't mention it." She'd lied to herself that it wouldn't matter.

"And you're still going to the interview, even with Mom and Haley both in the hospital?"

"This interview was hard enough to get. If I ask to reschedule it, they might decide they don't want to talk to me after all."

He didn't say anything for the longest time, and when he finally spoke up, his voice sounded strange. "I just can't believe you would still want to leave. After… everything."

"Logan, I—"

"I care about you, Caroline. More than I ever expected to care about anyone." His tone suggested he wasn't happy about the situation. "And as I told Matthew, I have lousy timing, what with Mom's condition and Haley's baby and even Dylan and Jenna's yet-to-be-announced, rescheduled wedding."

Caroline opened her mouth to interrupt him, to stop

the words that squeezed her heart like an angry fist, but Logan shook his head.

"Let me finish. This is about more than how I feel about you." He fisted his hands against the legs of his dress pants. "I think you care about me, too. We owe it to ourselves to explore the possibility of a real relationship between us. This could be the real thing. We'll never find out with you in Chicago and me in Markston."

Her heart raced. So this was what it was like to want something desperately and to be just as sure that it would be the worst thing in the world for her.

"I do...care about you." She choked on the words, as she was tempted to say what was really in her heart. "It's just complicated. I've told you before that I have these king-sized ambitions that will never mix with a home and family. I just lost sight of that for a little while."

"Stop it. You can keep on lying to yourself, but don't lie to me."

Caroline had just lifted her lukewarm tea from the table, and his words startled her so much that her hand jerked, sending light brown liquid sloshing over the side of the cup onto the carpet. Logan was up in a flash, hurrying into the kitchen and returning with a roll of paper towels. He sopped up the liquid. "Look. As good as new."

She nodded, sorry that their relationship could never be as good as new again. They would be blessed if they could salvage any sort of friendship from the train wreck she'd been responsible for creating.

He took the towels into the kitchen and tossed them in the garbage. When he returned, he sat in the same spot he'd been in before and turned to face her.

"I'm not lying to myself," she couldn't help saying

though she realized she was bringing up a subject again that she should allow to die.

"Aren't you?" He tilted his head and studied her. "You've been using your career aspirations as a way to hide from life. With that excuse, you can hide from relationships and from the chance that anyone would ever hurt you again."

"You've got it wrong." She didn't look up at him as she said it.

"I don't think so. You're talking to a master at avoiding relationships. I used to be, anyway. You're better than I ever was. At least I knew why I was doing it."

Until then, Caroline had been listening to his words, not quite believing but not able to deny what he'd said. Now, though, she was angry, and she couldn't help striking back.

"You think you know me, but you don't know anything about me." She crossed her arms as she faced him, her hands fisted beneath opposite elbows. "This is all so easy for you to say. You might have had to give up your safety net of always having a revolving door of first dates to build a relationship with one person, but no one has asked you to give up your *life* for a relationship."

"Is that what you think I'm asking you to do? What if I'm asking you to really *live* your life?"

"We've been on one date, and you're expecting me to move back to Markston. You're just like Kevin, expecting me to give up everything for you."

This time Logan stood up from the couch and started pacing, his anger visible in his jerky movements.

"That wasn't fair," she said in a quiet voice.

He stopped and looked back at her over his shoulder.

"No, it wasn't. From what you've said about him, I hope I'm nothing like him."

"But you did tell me you care about me, and then you're asking me to choose between you and the goals I've had all of my life. It's so easy for you to ask me to throw away all of my dreams."

"If that's what you think, then maybe you should go back to Chicago. You'll fulfill all your dreams there."

Instead of saying more, he stalked across the room to the slider, where he could stare outside. Caroline tried to see what he saw, but the darkness outside was obscured by fog as heavy as her heart. She'd made her decision, and she was prepared to live with it. So why did it feel as if she'd just made the biggest mistake of her life?

At the sound of the garage door opening, Caroline started. Dylan had been able to convince her mother to finally come home after all.

Trina came through the door in a rush as if Caroline were still a teenager and she'd broken the rules by having a boy in the house when no parent was home.

"Oh, good. You're still here, Logan," she managed though she sounded out of breath. "I wanted to talk to you two."

Caroline's blood went cold for the umpteenth time in a single day. What if she'd been having this self-ish conversation while Mrs. Warren's or Haley's health was taking a downturn? How would she ever forgive herself?

Logan turned back from the window and then strode toward her. "Are they both all right?"

"They're doing fine in our Lord's hands. The doctors are even cautiously optimistic about Amy's condition, and Haley's resting comfortably."

"You've had an awful lot to handle today, haven't you, Mom?" Caroline stood up and crossed to her mother, wrapping her arms around her though Trina would never have asked for a hug. She only hoped her mother benefited from it as much as she had.

"If everyone's okay, then why did you want to talk to us?" Logan wanted to know.

"I didn't get the chance to talk to either of you this morning about your new relationship, and this afternoon it was too crazy with postponing the wedding and—"

"It's okay, Mom. You don't have to say anything. We understood that you and Mrs. Warren didn't see this as a good match, and we know you had your reasons."

"No matter what we thought, I want to hear the whole story of how you ended up together."

Caroline couldn't help but look at her mother strangely. She didn't seem as upset about a relationship between the two of them as Caroline would have expected.

"It's a long story," Caroline began.

"It doesn't matter now," Logan added.

Trina frowned at them, looking as annoyed as she had that first day when the two of them argued over who should run the bakery. "Would you two listen to yourselves? I think we were right when we decided that you were the two most infuriating people who ever lived. What I'm trying to say is—"

But Logan must not have been ready to hear whatever she had to say because he waved a hand in front of her to interrupt her. "Don't worry, Mrs. Scott. There is not an *us*. There's nothing left to tell."

Chapter Fifteen

Early the next morning, while the Markston streets were still deserted, Logan unlocked back door of Amy's Elite Treats. It would have been a waste of time, anyway, for him stay in bed longer, telling himself sleep would eventually come.

For the first time in six weeks, his chest wasn't filled with anticipation over the prospect of seeing Caroline at the bakery. No use wasting energy on something that wouldn't be happening. She wouldn't be in today, and by afternoon, she would be out of Markston altogether.

Again a hollow hopelessness spread through his insides like low cloud cover on a dreary day. Had his life only now become this empty, or had it always been a void until Caroline had come along to magnify the vacuum? He shook his head. The answer to that question didn't matter. The only thing that did matter was that she wasn't with him.

So this was what it felt like to have his heart crushed. This must have been how his mother had felt when his father had left, and he wouldn't wish this kind of pain on his worst enemy. No matter how much he'd always worried that he might hurt someone the way his father had, Logan could admit to himself now that he'd dreaded this possibility even more.

But with Caroline he'd forgotten to be afraid, hadn't thought to take the most basic precautions to protect his heart. She'd made him feel invincible, and even now, even after he'd learned how bitter the taste of rejection could be, he didn't regret taking the chance.

He couldn't have resisted her if he'd tried, anyway. He'd been crazy about her from that first day when she'd marched into the bakery and announced her takeover bid.

He was to blame for her leaving. He'd known how difficult it had been for her to take a risk on him. After claiming he knew her better than anyone else did, he'd pushed her to relieve his own insecurities instead of respecting that she'd been upset over his mother's and Haley's conditions. He might have had her with him a few days longer, but instead he had sent her rushing back to Chicago two days before her big interview.

He glanced around the dark kitchen that appeared even emptier than usual with its pans and utensils all in their proper places. How would he ever be able to come to work here inputting inventory figures or oversee- ing wedding cake prep without wondering what Caro- line would have thought about a flour order or one of Kamie's or Margie's newest creations?

He might have learned that he wasn't like his father, but he'd behaved like Caroline's former fiancé. Given her history, how could he even have considered asking her to walk away from her life in Chicago for him? Could he really love her and yet ask her to give up so much for him?

If he hadn't been so demanding, he might have found a way for them to still have some sort of relationship once she returned to Chicago. Instead, she was gone for good, and he was alone, the way he deserved to be.

They were at an impasse, and he knew it. One would have to forfeit her dreams, or the other would have to give up his home and obligations. Neither was right or fair.

Lord, why did You lead me to Caroline, the most impossible woman who ever lived? And why now, the worst time for our families?

But even as he asked the questions in prayer, Logan realized he already knew the answers to them. This woman was the only one God had intended for him, and this was the one time he was ready to recognize it.

What had seemed like an impasse no longer felt like an impossibility. There had to be a solution, not necessarily an easy one but a solution nonetheless. Turning into the office, he powered up his mother's laptop. He had an Internet search to begin and only a few hours before the employees started arriving. He could only hope that some job opening in Chicago called for a forestry degree.

He understood that it might not be possible to overcome the obstacles that kept them apart or that Caroline might not think he was worth the effort, but he had to try.

Caroline paused to wipe her fingers along her lash lines before entering her second patient room of the morning. Haley hadn't bought any of her excuses for having swollen eyes any more than their mother had at the house so Caroline hoped Mrs. Warren would let her off easier.

Logan's mother had been too preoccupied to know anything about her son's budding romance, so Caroline didn't see any reason to tell her about it now that it had died before reaching full bloom.

"Hel-lo," Amy called out when she caught sight of Caroline in the doorway.

"Oh, you're awake." She hurried over to Amy's bed and bent to kiss her cheek. "You're looking so much better today. I'm so pleased that they already moved you to a regular room."

She lowered into the seat next to the bed and gripped Amy's hand between her two.

"More observation. Less machines."

"That's wonderful. Mom told me that doctors' concerns about a major stroke decrease with each day that passes."

Amy nodded. "They said that."

Logan's mother seemed to be watching her too closely, so Caroline glanced out the window. As dark and hopeless as she felt today, it should have been raining outside, yet the sunshine and clear skies were relentless.

"Haley?"

"She's fine," Caroline assured her. "Her OB told Matthew he could take her home later today, but she'll be on bed rest until she delivers."

"Tough with Lizzie."

Caroline nodded. "Yes, it will be tough, but we'll all pitch in to— I mean, the family will help her out."

"Not you?"

Caroline was surprised that Mrs. Warren had picked up on the layers in her comment. She'd expected the mini-strokes to cause a major setback in the woman's recovery, but it didn't appear as if Amy had lost much ground.

Amy didn't ask another question, but she stared for so long that Caroline found herself filling the silence with an explanation.

"I have to get back to Chicago. I have a promising interview on Wednesday, and I want to get back to my apartment so I can prepare for it. I already packed the car. I just wanted to stop by to visit you and Haley before I got on the road."

Caroline glanced out the window again and back at Amy. "It's been nice being here, but I'm looking forward to going home again."

"Home...is Markston."

Caroline narrowed her gaze at Logan's mother, convinced the woman had confused what she was saying. "No. Remember, Mrs. Warren. I live in Chicago. That's home. I've only been visiting Markston."

"Logan?"

At the sound of his name, Caroline blinked, and her throat clogged with emotion. She reminded herself that Mrs. Warren was the only member of their families who hadn't seen Logan and her together. With Mrs. Warren's clipped speech patterns, she could have been asking from any number of things, so Caroline tried to guess which one.

"Are you asking if he'll be in the bakery today? I'm sure he will." She cleared her throat. "I won't be there after this, but he's fully capable of running the business alone. He always was."

"Not...asking that."

"Then are you wanting to know if he'll be in to visit

you today? He probably will. He'll want to celebrate how well you're doing."

But Amy only shook her head.

"I'm sorry, Mrs. Warren. I don't understand what you're asking."

Amy pulled her hand from between Caroline's two and then patted the young woman's arm. "Logan and you."

"Oh. I didn't know you knew." She wanted to demand to know *how* she knew, but the news about the two of them hadn't been a secret. Any one of their siblings could have mentioned something to Amy when they'd taken turns visiting with her.

Caroline crossed her arms in a protective self-hug. "Yes, Logan and I thought there might be possibilities between us, but we realized we weren't good together."

"Wrong. My son…is in love…with you."

Caroline could only stare at her. It was one of the clearest comments she'd heard Mrs. Warren make since the initial stroke. Logan hadn't even said those specific words to Caroline himself, but her heart ached with the knowledge that his mother was right.

The tears she promised herself she wouldn't cry came out of nowhere and streamed down her face. She wiped at them, but the tears kept coming.

"Don't cry," Amy said, reaching over to touch her arm.

"I don't know what's wrong with me." Finding a box of tissues on the table next to the bed, Caroline pulled out several and started dabbing.

"Think you do."

Wadding a tissue in her fist, Caroline looked back to

her. "You're right. I love him, too. I haven't even told him that. But I have my own life. There are so many things I've worked for, all these goals I haven't met yet."

Mrs. Warren nodded as if it all made sense to her. "Will you be...fulfilled...to have it all—" She stopped in middle of her question as if to regroup or find the words and then she tried again. "If there's no one...to share it with?"

All those words must have been tiring for Mrs. Warren, because she reached her good hand up to rub her eyes.

"You're tired, sweetie." Caroline brushed Amy's hair back from her face. "Why don't you rest for a while. I'll get going now."

"Logan?" she asked one last time.

Caroline shook her head. "I don't know."

After hugging Amy, Caroline hurried out of the room, somehow managing not to run. Once she was in the hallway, she sagged against the wall, Mrs. Warren's speech ringing in her ears. Her mouth felt dry and her pulse pounded inside her head.

Did she really want to "have it all"? No. She didn't even care about the job search she'd been pursuing with the desperation of one who had something to prove. Logan was right. She hadn't been trying to have it all. She'd been *hiding* from it all. Running and hiding.

"I don't want it all."

Caroline didn't realize she'd spoken aloud until a nurse passing by in blue scrubs turned to look at her.

"Excuse me," she said with a shrug.

When the woman continued past her, Caroline straightened and started down the hall to the elevator.

Once outside the hospital, she hurried to her car but couldn't help slowing as she neared it.

Even with most of her things in the trunk, she still had two boxes in the backseat. Mostly yearbooks and forensics trophies that her mother had been storing for her in the new house's tiny attic. The packed car couldn't have been a more obvious sign that she was ready to run again. This time she'd been planning to run from Logan and from feelings she felt for him that were just as scary as the prospect of being alone.

But she didn't want to run anymore, and she didn't want to hide. At once, the thought of the four-hour drive back to Chicago exhausted her, and the prospect of returning to that dark apartment didn't make her outlook any brighter. She couldn't even muster any enthusiasm for her upcoming interview.

What was wrong with her? If she got this job, she would be right back on the corporate ladder, not on the bottom rung, either. She was so confused. This used to be what she wanted, but she wanted different things now, and Logan was at the center of all those things.

Unlocking her car door, she climbed inside and put the keys in the ignition, but she didn't start the engine. *If there's no one to share it with.* As Mrs. Warren's words played again in her head, Caroline rested her forehead against the steering wheel, gripping it with both hands. The words cut her more deeply than she ever could have imagined.

She realized now that she could have all the success in the world, but it wouldn't feel like success if she couldn't share her life with Logan. But the damage was already done. She'd walked away from him just as his father had. She couldn't even imagine how badly she'd hurt him. How could she ever expect him to consider building a relationship with her after that? Even if he could forgive her, and she doubted he could, he would never be able to trust her not to leave again.

Why had she realized too late that she loved him more than she loved all her big plans? And she did love him. She wanted the best for him whether or not they could ever be together.

Caroline lifted her head and stared out the windshield. "'Love bears all things, believes all things, hopes all things, endures all things.'"

It took her a few seconds to realize she was quoting a memory verse from her childhood and only a few seconds longer to place it at as part of the passage from I Corinthians Chapter 13 that Jenna had selected for her wedding. Since when did Caroline quote Scripture? But the answer to that question was as clear as the image of the man always in her thoughts and embedded in her heart.

She was changed for having known Logan. His perspective on the world was different from hers, yet it had encouraged her to examine hers. His dedication to his faith had inspired her to open her heart again to her own.

How ironic that she'd thought she was helping *him* when she'd first shown up at the bakery. All along, he'd been the one helping her. It had taken her a while to recognize the blessing and be grateful. Though they'd agreed once not to keep score, she still wished there were something she could do to show her gratitude.

But then the idea struck her, so perfect and so simple that she couldn't believe she hadn't realized it before. It didn't matter whether she and Logan could ever be together again. There was still something she could do for him and for his family. She'd always been focused on her own dreams, but suddenly it had become important for her to support someone else's.

With her decision made, Caroline turned the ignition, the wheels in her thoughts turning long before she put the car in Drive. So much would need to be done once she reached her mother's house. Checking into ending her lease was only the beginning.

She glanced in the rearview mirror at the boxes in the backseat. Her mother wouldn't be able to rid her attic of those, after all.

"Lord, let all the pieces fall into place," she began to pray, "if it is Your will. Amen."

She wouldn't let herself get her hopes up about Logan's reaction to her decision to stay. That was in God's hands. Right now she could only worry about her mom's best friend and a bakery called Amy's Elite Treats, because for the first time in a long time, she was absolutely certain she was doing the right thing.

Chapter Sixteen

Logan took a deep breath to calm himself as he climbed out of his truck and trudged through the hospital parking lot. Glancing around, he caught sight of Dylan's and Matthew's vehicles parked side by side in the south lot.

Maybe they should have met at the bakery as he'd first suggested, but Matthew had been right to mention that they would want to talk to their mother about it as soon as the three of them came up with a plan. Giving the news in person was the least he could do given that he'd begged for the chance to take over care for his mother's business, and now he needed to make them understand why he had to walk away from that responsibility.

As he stepped on the walkway leading to the main entrance, something in his peripheral vision caught his attention. At the sight of the familiar-looking car, his breath caught. Caroline? Because he couldn't be sure it belonged to her, he crossed back to look at the rear of the vehicle, his heart beating furiously. As soon as he saw the Illinois plates, Logan jogged up to the hospital's main entrance.

Once inside the building, he held his pace to a brisk walk, but he couldn't get to the waiting room soon enough. He skidded to a halt when he reached it, seeing only Matthew, Jenna and Dylan sitting at the table in the corner.

It felt like a cruel joke that someone from Illinois, driving the same model of car as Caroline, would have shown up at the hospital tonight, but that only meant he was back to Plan A. He continued across the room but at a slower pace.

"Oh, Logan," Jenna called out in a loud voice. "There you are."

When his brothers turned back to him, wearing those goofy grins, he looked around the room for whatever they'd found so funny. Emerging from the snack area carrying two sodas was Mrs. Scott with Lizzie trailing behind her. And following those two was the woman whose face was a permanent fixture in his best dreams.

Mrs. Scott stopped so quickly that Lizzie ran into her back, and then she moved off to the side so that Caroline had an unimpaired view. He knew the exact moment she saw him because she stopped, frozen.

In four long paces, he'd made it over to her. "What are you doing here?"

She swallowed visibly and then indicated the table with a gesture of her hand. "I'm with your family."

"I mean why are you not back in Chicago already?"

"I planned a meeting with them."

As much as he hated looking away from her, Logan

turned his head to Caroline's mother for confirmation. "I thought *I* planned this meeting."

Trina smiled and held her hands wide. "Well, isn't this wonderful, because technically you're both right. You both called a meeting."

Logan turned back to Caroline. "I don't understand."

"This was supposed to be a surprise," Caroline said.

"Did you decide to wait until tomorrow to go back? I know your interview isn't until Wednesday—"

"I canceled the interview."

He looked into her eyes for answers but didn't find any. "Now I really don't understand."

"I'm not going back to Chicago."

Logan blinked. "You're staying in Markston?"

When Caroline nodded, his pulse raced just as it had on his jog from the parking lot. "But why?" He wanted to smack himself for asking it. Did he really want her to think he'd wanted her to leave?

"I've been meeting with your brothers and your future sister-in-law here about the possibility of my managing the bakery long-term." Caroline held up her hand when he tried to interrupt her. "This way your mother will be able to return to work in whatever capacity she is capable of. It will be good for her to know she can still be a part of the business."

Logan started shaking his head, but Caroline continued on, as if she was determined to get her argument out before he could stop her.

"Now don't get me wrong. The business will always be Mrs. Warren's. I'll run it however she sees fit. And you can pay me whatever you're able. I'll supplement that income by getting a second part-time job and using some of my savings."

He glanced over to the table for assistance from his brothers, but they appeared to be having a great time watching the exchange that he clearly wasn't winning. Finally, she took a breath, giving him the chance to get in a word or two.

"But why would you want to do this? What about your career? What about the glass ceiling? You can't give up all of that just to work in my mom's bakery."

"Sure I can," she said lightly before becoming serious. "Why was it okay for you to give up your career to run the business, but it's not okay for me to do it?"

"A lot of reasons," he answered, but then he found it difficult to say them to her. How could he tell her that he believed her goals were somehow more valid than his? "But mostly it's that I can't allow you to give up your dreams for my mother's or even mine."

"What if I were to tell you that I have different dreams now and that they all involve living in Markston and being near family?"

Logan tried to keep a straight face. This all sounded too perfect, and so he was waiting for the bubble to burst. "I would question your sanity."

"Well, don't. I am perfectly lucid." She stopped and planted her hands on her hips. "And you know how stubborn I can be when I want something."

"Yeah, a mule has nothing on you." He shook his head. "I just don't understand why you're doing this."

Caroline held up her hands as if to signify how simple the answer was. "I want to make sure that the world's best park biologist isn't forced to leave the beautiful outdoors, where he belongs."

Logan could only stare at her, finally understanding that she was doing this for him. She might as well have answered his question, "because I love you." It all became clear to him now.

"Then it's settled," Trina chimed in, having been uncharacteristically quiet for the past few minutes. "Can you believe these two are still arguing over who is going to run the bakery?"

Logan hadn't noticed his brothers, Jenna and Lizzie moving closer, but suddenly they had joined Caroline's mother and crowded around them.

But Caroline wasn't paying attention to the others. She was still studying Logan with a perplexed expression on her face. "Wait. You said you called a meeting, too. Why did you do it?"

"Yeah, Logan," Matthew chimed with a chuckle. "Tell her why you called this meeting."

Dylan elbowed Jenna. "This is really getting good. We should have brought popcorn for this."

"Glad we could entertain you." Logan frowned at his brother before turning back to Caroline. Obviously, the others had left her in the dark about discussions he'd had earlier with his brothers just as they hadn't told him about Caroline's offer to stay. "I brought everyone together so I could quit at the bakery."

Trina touched his shoulder. "Now, Logan Warren, that isn't exactly the case, is it?" She turned her head to Caroline to explain. "Yes, he said he wanted to step away from the day-to-day operations, but he said he could continue doing all of the books from Chicago."

Caroline swallowed, sure she must have heard wrong. "Chicago? You're moving to Chicago?"

"There's a good chance, anyway," Logan told her. "I've scheduled two interviews for Friday."

"But you told me you couldn't picture yourself living anywhere but in Markston. And you didn't want to leave your work at the park."

Logan shrugged, grinning. "It turns out those are only a place and a job. I can live anywhere and work anywhere as long as..."

He let his words trail away as if he was suddenly aware that he'd been about to say private things in front of a crowd.

What had he been about to say? Caroline couldn't believe her ears. Logan was willing to give up his life in Markston and the work he loved for *her?* She was even more convinced that she'd done the right thing by choosing to stay.

"Hey, Matthew, didn't Haley just call to say she was being released?" Trina called out. "Why don't we all go upstairs and collect her?"

Caroline would have kissed her mother right then as Trina led the others from the room, but she found herself rooted where she was. It was as if her whole life had led her to this spot and to the next words Logan Warren had to say.

"They're gone."

Her trance broken, she couldn't help but to grin. It wasn't exactly the dialogue she would have written in her dreams, but this was real life.

She cleared her throat, though she still couldn't remove the thickness of emotion from her voice. "You were saying you could live anywhere as long as..."

"As long as I can be with the woman I love."

Her breath caught as she heard the exact words that

dreams were made of, that reality made perfect. Logan didn't even hesitate. He dropped to his knee right in the middle of the waiting room. Caroline realized that hospital visitors and personnel had to be passing through the room, but she didn't care about anything except this moment and this man she'd been waiting for all her life. When he reached for her hand, Caroline, who did nothing without a plan, offered it without a second thought.

"I'm in love with you, Caroline Scott. You're the one. I've been spinning my wheels for years, going on too many first dates and not knowing why." He smiled at her. "Now I know. I was waiting for you."

He held her hand between his two. "The only way my life will be perfect is if you will agree to a lifetime of first dates with me. Will you marry me?"

"I thought you'd never ask."

At once, Logan was on his feet, and Caroline was in his arms. Exactly where she always should have been. When he lowered his mouth to hers, Caroline lifted up on her toes so she could meet him halfway. His kiss felt like a promise fulfilled, a prayer answered. He tilted his head and kept right on kissing her, touching her heart with every brush of his lips.

When someone cleared her throat, Logan and Caroline stepped back from each other and turned to see the crowd gathered next to the elevator. Several members of the group broke out in applause, and Matthew and Dylan started fanning themselves.

"Whew, it's getting warm in here," Dylan said with a laugh.

"All right. Everyone out of the way." Trina's authoritative voice came from behind the younger members of the family.

The others separated, and Trina stood there with not one but two wheelchairs. Matthew and Lizzie crossed back to push Haley's chair, while Trina pushed Mrs. Warren in the second chair.

Logan stepped back but still held on to Caroline's hand.

Once they were all together in the middle of the waiting room, Trina crouched next to Amy.

"Oh, we're too late." Trina snapped her fingers. "We missed it."

"But he asked…right?" Amy wanted to know.

The side of Logan's mouth lifted. "Yes, Mom, I asked. And she said yes. Well, sort of."

At his sidelong glance, Caroline grinned. "Yes."

Logan smiled back and then, stepping over to his mother, crouched in front of her wheelchair. "Are you okay, Mom? Are you sure you should be up and about?"

"Don't worry," Trina told him. "I got permission from her doctor. She's going to be transferred back to the rehab center tomorrow, but I couldn't let her miss this."

Caroline looked back and forth between the two women. "This?"

Trina grinned. "The fruits of our labor, of course. Our third and final matchmaking plan was a success."

"What?" Logan and Caroline chorused. They looked at each other in shock and then turned back to their mothers.

Her mother was chuckling, and Caroline was almost

convinced that she saw the beginning of a smile on Mrs. Warren's lips.

Caroline drew her eyebrows together. "How can that be? Logan is about the last man in the world you two ever would have chosen for me." She glanced at him apologetically, but he only shrugged.

"That's what we thought at first. Remember, we did try a few others earlier." Trina shrugged as she glanced over at Matthew and Dylan. "But then we realized that nobody *but* Amy's Logan would be perfect for my Caroline."

Logan shook his head. "I don't believe it. Caroline and I found each other. You're just taking the credit for bringing us together."

Trina lifted a shoulder and lowered it. "Mothers never reveal all their secrets." She reached down and brushed Amy's silver hair.

Then Amy surprised them by speaking up. "God does work...in myster-ious ways."

"You're right, Mom," Logan told her. "And His ways are perfect."

With that he leaned over to kiss Caroline, and she smiled against his lips. Yes. Perfect.

Caroline blotted her lipstick and adjusted her veil in the mirror and then glanced over at Jenna, who was touching up her makeup. Her gaze went to her hand, and she was still surprised to see the lovely diamond solitaire and shiny gold band together for the first time.

"Hurry up, will you?" Caroline said. "Everyone's waiting for us to cut the cakes."

Jenna grinned at her reflection. "Relax, Miss Type-A.

Or should I say Mrs. Type-A? We've already made it to the chapel."

She hummed the tune to "The Chapel of Love" until Caroline finally took a deep breath and grinned back at her.

"That's Mrs. Warren to you," Caroline said. "Okay, Mrs. Warren?"

It had been a whirlwind eight-week engagement to make their wedding on the last Saturday in August, but as far as Caroline was concerned, it had been entirely too long. She'd been so excited to finally be Logan's wife.

"I still can't believe you decided not to keep your maiden name. Or at least hyphenate." Turning away from the mirror, Jenna glanced at her quizzically. "What happened to my feminist sister?"

"She's still here." Caroline brushed a hand down the front of the simple silk bodice of her wedding gown. "But I couldn't go around with a different last name than my sisters, could I?"

"You know, most married sisters actually do have different last names."

"Oh. Right. But then they're not the Scott sisters, either."

They stepped together for a warm hug. As they pulled apart, Caroline held on to Jenna's arms.

"Thank you again for sharing your wedding day with us. I know how important it was for you to plan an incredible wedding."

"Are you kidding? Today couldn't be more incredible."

Someone knocked on the door, interrupting them.

"Are you ladies coming?" Haley called from outside.

With one last peek at the mirror, Jenna and Caroline continued out into the hall. Haley stood there, looking radiant in the bridesmaid's dress that Caroline originally was supposed to have worn. It had been hemmed for Haley's more petite height, but it had required no major alterations.

"Have I told you how fabulous you look?" Caroline told Haley as she hugged her. "Little Evan isn't even a month old, and you already can wear a fitted dress like that?"

"Thanks." She lifted on her tiptoes to kiss her sister's cheek. "But I can tell you this. I'm not outshining either of the brides. You're the two belles of the ball. Now can we get back to the reception?"

As Jenna and Caroline reentered the hall, their new husbands came over to escort them over to the two cakes, different but complementary designs made by Margie and Kamie just for each couple.

Logan leaned close and kissed his bride's cheek. "Are you having second thoughts?"

Caroline rolled her eyes at him. "No. Never."

"I'll remind you of that after I smear wedding cake all over your face."

"You'd better not or I'll—"

"What will you do, Mrs. Warren?" he said with a chuckle.

After they finished cutting the cake and feeding each other a bite—with Logan setting Caroline's primly on her tongue—they crossed the room to the table where their mothers were seated.

"Well, you all did it." Trina stood and lifted her cheek for Caroline's kiss and then Logan's.

"Yes, we did," Dylan called out as he led Jenna over to the group. Both bent to hug Amy in her wheelchair.

The two couples switched sides so that Jenna and Dylan could greet Trina and Logan and Caroline could hug Amy. At the sound of a baby crying, they all turned to see Matthew pulling a bottle from a diaper bag and popping it in Evan's hungry mouth. Lizzie was oblivious to it all, dancing around the room in her pretty flower girl dress.

Trina glanced across the room at the pair of cakes. "If those cakes are any indicator, everything's going well at the bakery."

"It will be even better when Mrs. Warren starts back next month," Caroline told her.

"Don't know...about that." But Amy smiled as she said it, and her hand went up to touch her hair.

Logan stepped over to his mother and patted her shoulder. "It will be great when you're back. I sure wish I could be there more, but it's good being back at the park, as well."

"Don't worry about him. He doesn't have to miss the cakes too much," Caroline said. "We're both doing well in our second cake-decorating class, but he's still better than I am with decorating skills."

Logan shrugged. "I have to be better than her at something."

Dylan and Logan went over to the buffet table to bring slices of cake for everyone, and when they returned, they had Frank Kellam with them. He, too, was carrying party plates filled with cake, and he handed the first one to Trina. Caroline knew she had to be mistaken, but she was almost certain her mother was blushing.

"Well, Mr. Kellam, it's so nice to see you again," Jenna said, grinning over her at her mother.

Trina must have missed the look because she didn't frown back.

The older gentleman kissed Jenna's cheek and shook Dylan's hand. "It was a lovely wedding, you two." He turned Logan and Caroline. "And you, too."

Logan shook his hand. "I hear it's been a good day for you, as well."

Mr. Kellam grinned like child who'd just been given candy. "Yes, it has." He touched Trina's arm and turned back to her daughters. "Your mother has finally agreed to have coffee with me."

"Oh, she has, has she?" Haley said as she approached, rocking the baby in her arms.

Trina shook her head, clearly embarrassed. "It's no big deal."

"Whatever you say, Mom," Caroline said.

"No big deal?" Mr. Kellam asked, easily fitting in with the Warren-Scott family humor. "I thought she would never agree to go out with me. But Amy told me—"

He stopped himself, but not before Trina jerked her head to look at him, her gaze narrowed.

"Oh. I wasn't supposed to say that." He glanced around nervously.

Logan grinned as he turned back to Amy. "Mother, have you been matchmaking again?"

"Not me," Amy answered and then turned to wipe her mouth with a napkin.

"Amy…?" Trina studied her.

"Somebody had…to make sure you…weren't alone," she said without a hint of an apology.

"Amy told me Trina would be a tough one, but I wasn't to take no for an answer," Mr. Kellam said. "And I didn't."

They all shared a laugh over the matchmaker who'd just been matched. "Oh, you," Trina said, smiling. "Just wait a few months. We'll have to start looking for someone for you." She paused, thinking. "What about Max Carlson or Bill White?"

They all laughed again. When the laughter died down, Logan moved through the crowd to Caroline and drew her into his arms.

"Happy?" He brushed his lips across her brow.

"Absolutely." Not worrying about the others around them, she turned her head so they could share a sweet kiss before she drew back. "Do you think this was what our moms had in mind when they started this matchmaking business?"

"Maybe something like it, but as your mom said, 'God does have a sense of humor.' It didn't end up quite the way they planned." He kissed one of her cheeks and then the other before dropping a third kiss on her nose.

She smiled up at him. "And He knew exactly what He was doing."

Logan lowered his head and kissed Caroline again. His kisses felt like a series of promises. Of love, laughter and family. Of forever.

* * * * *

Dear Reader,

I have never been known for my patience. Just ask my high school journalism adviser. I walked into newspaper class my freshman year, already planning for when I would be editor. I later held that position for my last two years of high school, but in that and in many other parts of my life I have struggled with waiting for things to happen in God's time.

But over the years, I have finally learned that God's time is perfect.

Of all the heroines in the WEDDING BELL BLESS-INGS miniseries, I relate the most to Caroline, who is driven to achieve and impatient for results. For Caroline, the need for success is tangled with her desire to hide from life, but she must learn that the answers to all of her questions will come if she is only patient and waits for God's will in His time. Logan comes into Caroline's life when she least expects it, and the timing is perfect.

I pray for you, my readers, to have patience to wait for God's perfect time.

I love hearing from readers and may be contacted through my Web site at www.danacorbit.com or through regular mail at P.O. Box 2251, Farmington Hills, MI 48333-2251.

Dana Corbit

QUESTIONS FOR DISCUSSION

1. What subject does Caroline bring up every time Logan gets too close and makes her nervous? How does this subject distance her from him?

2. Why is Caroline so bothered by Reverend Boggs's sermon on her first Sunday back in Markston? Why is *Mark* 10 such a problem for her?

3. Logan correctly assumes that it is a man who caused Caroline to rule out the possibility of ever marrying. Who hurt Caroline, and how did that hurt affect her?

4. Why is Logan afraid of ever building a long-term relationship? How has he avoided committed relationships with women so far?

5. Logan loves to spend time in prayer and feels closer to God in a scenic spot in the state park where he works. Is there anyplace where you go alone to pray? Is there a place other than church where you feel closest to God?

6. Why does Jenna pick out such a special bridesmaid's dress for Caroline? Who ultimately wears this dress?

7. How does Logan's birth order influence how he was affected by his father's desertion when he was only ten? Are children in the same family really affected differently when their parents divorce?

8. Why does Trina Scott turn down Frank Kellam when he first invites her to lunch?

9. Caroline must deal with the working woman's concept of having it all. Can a woman really have it all without at least one part of her life having to give?

10. Amy Warren's stroke is central to this story. Why is Logan unwilling to even think about the fact that his mother would not be able to return to work at her bakery?

11. Logan tells Caroline she is hiding. What is she hiding from, and what is she using to shield herself?

12. Caroline believes she is saving Logan when she offers to help run the bakery, but Logan often ends up saving her. In what ways does Logan help Caroline?

13. Have you ever known someone who suffered a stroke like Amy? Was that person able to recover and live a productive life? What might you say to someone in a situation like that?

14. Caroline has trouble fitting regular church attendance into her life in Chicago because she works Sundays. How important is attending regular services to living a Christian life?

15. Who is ultimately responsible for matchmaking Caroline and Logan?

Love Inspired®

TITLES AVAILABLE NEXT MONTH

Available August 31, 2010

BABY MAKES A MATCH
Chatam House
Arlene James

DOCTOR RIGHT
Alaskan Bride Rush
Janet Tronstad

SHELTER OF HOPE
New Friends Street
Lyn Cote

LOVE FINDS A HOME
Mirror Lake
Kathryn Springer

MADE TO ORDER FAMILY
Ruth Logan Herne

COURTING RUTH
Hannah's Daughters
Emma Miller

Enjoy a sneak peek at fan favorite Molly O'Keefe's
Harlequin Superromance miniseries,
THE NOTORIOUS O'NEILLS, *with*
TYLER O'NEILL'S REDEMPTION,
available September 2010
only from Harlequin Superromance.

Police chief Juliette Tremblant recognized the shape of the man strolling down the street—in as calm and leisurely fashion as if it were the middle of the day rather than midnight. She slowed her car, convinced her eyes were playing tricks on her. It had been a long time since Tyler O'Neill had been seen in this town.

As she pulled to a stop at the curb, he turned toward her, and her heart about stopped.

"What the hell are you doing here, Tyler?"

"Well, if it isn't Juliette Tremblant." He made his way over to her, then leaned down so he could look her in the eye. He was close enough to touch.

Juliette was not, repeat, *not* going to touch Tyler O'Neill. Not with her fingers. Not with a ten-foot pole. There would be no touching. Which was too bad, since it was the only way she was ever going to convince herself the man standing in front of her—as rumpled and heart-stoppingly handsome now as he'd been at sixteen—was real.

And not a figment of all her furious revenge dreams.

"What are you doing back in Bonne Terre?" she asked.

"The manor is sitting empty," Tyler said and shrugged, as though his arriving out of the blue after ten years was casual. "Seems like someone should be watching over the family home."

"You?" She laughed at the very notion of him being here for any unselfish reason. "Please."

He stared at her for a second, then smiled. Her heart fluttered against her chest—a small mechanical bird powered by that smile.

"You're right." But that cryptic comment was all he offered.

Juliette bit her lip against the other questions.

Why did you go?

Why didn't you write? Call?

What did I do?

But what would be the point? Ten years of silence were all the answer she really needed.

She had sworn off feeling anything for this man long ago. Yet one look at him and all the old hurt and rage resurfaced as though they'd been waiting for the chance. That made her mad.

She put the car in gear, determined not to waste another minute thinking about Tyler O'Neill. "Have a good night, Tyler," she said, liking all the cool "go screw yourself" she managed to fit into those words.

It seems Juliette has an old score to settle with Tyler.
Pick up TYLER O'NEILL'S REDEMPTION
to see how he makes it up to her.
Available September 2010,
only from Harlequin Superromance.

MARGARET WAY

introduces

The lives & loves of
Australia's most powerful family

Growing up in the spotlight hasn't been easy, but the two
Rylance heirs, Corin and his sister, Zara, have come of age
and are ready to claim their inheritance. Though they are
privileged, proud and powerful, they are about to discover
that there are some things money can't buy....

Look for:

Australia's Most Eligible Bachelor
Available September

Cattle Baron Needs a Bride
Available October

HR17679